"ARE YOU TELLING ME I'M TOO STAID?"

Johanna snuggled up next to Jonathan on the over-stuffed couch. She tilted her head to glance up at him. "Exactly," she said as the credits started to roll.

He lowered his head, giving her time to pull back if she wanted to. Johanna didn't want to and in seconds, his lips met hers, firm, insistent, overpowering.

There weren't many incidents in life that stole Johanna's breath. Jonathan's kiss did—a tidal wave of emotions swamped her every time she neared him.

Jonathan eased his lips from hers, knowing he should stop this before he went too far.

Johanna was Karina's friend, but he couldn't picture her as only his sister's friend any longer. He saw her as a woman—a woman he wanted in his bed. A woman he longed to be with—to make love with.

D1601406

INTIMATE SECRETS

CANDICE POARCH

BET Publications, LLC
www.msbet.com
www.arabesquebooks.com

ARABESQUE BOOKS are published by

BET Publications, LLC
c/o BET BOOKS
One BET Plaza
1900 W Place NE
Washington, D.C. 20018-1211

First Printing: September, 1999
10 9 8 7 6 5 4 3 2 1

Printed in the United States of America

DEDICATION

To my sister,
Evangeline Poarch Jones.
Thank you.

ACKNOWLEDGMENTS

There were so many people who helped with the research I needed for this book. Thank you George Walker, Marvin Goode, Donald Drain and Carole Thompson.

I extend a special thank you to Nicolette Jardine for her wonderful work in developing my web page and in providing publicity material.

As always, a heartfelt thank you to my critique partner, Sandy Rangel.

PROLOGUE

Johanna Jones stared unbelievably at the computer screen for five whole seconds before she emitted a sharp gasp and a shrill screech mere seconds before Tyrone, her current beau, bellowed at something on the tube. Week after week, he'd watched the Redskins with the kind of exuberance she'd yet to see in their most passionate encounter.

Perhaps somebody made a touchdown or something but she couldn't be concerned just now when her twenty-six-year dream finally leaped within her grasp. Her several thousand shares of stock in sixteen companies had collectively risen enough for her to purchase the Nottoway Inn, the hotel she'd craved to own since she was seven years old.

Her whole body tingled with the thrill of her success. Her stocks had just reached their highest peak right along with the Dow Jones average.

A few minutes later, Tyrone halted his "yeas," and "all rights," and the springs stopped squeaking on the ancient couch she'd bought at Marlo's long enough for him to say, "Everything all right over there, baby? You in the mood?"

She paused, took deep breaths for calm and responded with, "I'm just fine . . . just fine," in what she hoped was a normal voice. Her back was still presented to him.

Clasping her hands tightly together to still the trembling reverberating through her body, her eyes remained affixed to the computer screen. For several minutes, that could have been a half hour for all she knew, she sat transfixed.

Slowly her world came into focus again. The commentator's play by play description of the game and Tyrone's voice were the predominate sounds. Slowly she turned to stare at Tyrone. Now slumped in the left corner of her sofa, he tilted his head to swallow huge gulps of Heineken, so intent on his football game that a bit dribbled from one corner of his mouth, marking a trail down his chin unnoticed.

"That's the way!" he bellowed and half rose from the seat, punching the air with his fist.

His hair, which he fastidiously combed into a neat style, stood at peaks where his fingers must have raked over his head, and he didn't care. Studying his excitement, Johanna determined that the thrill exploding through her caused by her rising portfolio was a lot like the passion Tyrone felt for his football game.

For several weeks, Tyrone had tried his best to convince her that it was time to get married. For once, Johanna longed for a man who would arouse her senses as much as her portfolio on its best day. That man wasn't Tyrone.

How could she even consider marriage to a man when the thrill of being in his arms didn't begin to compare to the exhilaration she'd just experienced. And this time, she didn't have to fake it.

She was quite fond of the man, and he was kind, but their affection was not the sort to induce wild, passionate yearnings in her.

Then she remembered Jonathan Blake—her idol as a teenager. He was probably graying now and beginning to lose his looks, not that she chose men by outward appearance. But he'd certainly made her heart dance with excitement when she was a teenager, though he never treated her as more than his kid sister's friend.

CHAPTER 1

"Johanna . . . ?" Languidly, Smith rose from his rocker on the front porch where his collie, Travis, rested beside him with his ears perked. Suddenly, the dog rose. With quick leaps, which was unusual for him, Travis descended the porch steps to greet Johanna Jones who rewarded him by scratching him behind his fluffy ears.

"How are you, old boy?" Johanna said to the fifteen-year-old collie. Travis rewarded her with two staccato barks and nuzzled closer for more attention. He knew the softy before him would give him his heart's desire.

Laughing, Johanna glanced at Smith. The man held his cap in his hand, showing off his sparse gray hair mussed from the cap. The man and the house both looked weather-beaten—Smith with sun-tortured lines, from too many hours fishing on the Nottoway, marking his features; the house with peeling paint falling away bit by bit.

Smith cleared his throat twice, shifted from one

foot to the other, looking around in desperate, quick gestures. Even though his first name was Collier, half of Nottoway was unaware of that fact. He'd been called Smith well before Johanna was even born. Today, he seemed agitated by her presence. Johanna looked fondly at the older man.

"What is it, Smith?" she asked, weary from working most of the day before she made the three-hour drive from Alexandria, Virginia, to Nottoway.

"The contractor ran into some trouble," he said. "They can't get some of the supplies on schedule so it's slowing things up." He turned his cap, which held hordes of fishing lures, round and round in his weathered and scarred hands. "I know you're running on a tight schedule, but these things happen." He shrugged his shoulders.

"What's slowing the supplies?" Johanna asked. The hotel needed to open soon and start producing an income. The opening couldn't be delayed.

"Well . . ." he started then gave up. "Confounded, Johanna, you need to talk to the contractor." Smith slapped the cap on his leg. "He should have called you by now." Irritated, he frowned at her. "He'll explain it all to you tomorrow," Smith told her.

Johanna took a deep breath. Smith hated dealing with the refurbishment. He only attended to it because Johanna had a job at a hotel in DC and couldn't get away. She was grateful to him for staying as long as he did. "Tell me what's going on first, please." Travis was crawling up her side by now. Johanna moved and sat on one of the creaky steps leading to the porch. Travis immediately put his forelegs on her lap and snuggled his head closer.

Smith sighed and returned to his rocker. "The contractor said he's having trouble getting some of the special molding you requested and a couple of other items. I tried to hurry him along, but I don't deal too well with that kind of stuff." He slapped his cap on his knee. "I'm just glad you're a day early. Nearly about drove me crazy with all the banging, stirring up and carrying on. Millions of questions to answer. Hundreds of county approvals," he grunted. "Almighty. I don't see how you can stand it."

"But I took care of most of that the last time I was here," Johanna said. "I got the county approvals. I approved everything with the contractor." The plan was to take as much of the pressure off Smith as she could. "He promised . . . "

"You know how projects like this are. It never goes as planned." He paused, a light appearing in his wintry eyes. "That hotel sure is beautiful, though. Looks better than it did when I was a child. By then it had already started to decline. You've done good, gal." He looked as if he were glancing back in time. "You seen it yet?"

"Not yet." Johanna threw the old man a warm glance, appreciating his approval. Since she was a child, Smith talked of how much he enjoyed his fishing and how he could hardly wait to get away from Nottoway, in the winters for better fishing. He'd remained at the hotel until she could buy it from him. "I appreciate your staying on to look after things until I could move here. Thank you," she said. "This means more to me than you'll ever know."

"Shucks gal, won't nothing. But deg gonnit, you got your work cut out for you." He took the cap off his head again and slapped it against his thigh. "All those people milling about. It's going to be a busy place. Just like it was when I was a boy. Even better. You don't have the Depression to contend with."

Johanna smiled. "Is my cabin finished, at least? Do I have a place to live?"

"Yeah, I'll get your key." He got up from his rocker, walked slowly on the porch, boards creaking with every other step.

As he entered the old white clapboard house, Johanna glanced around her. A weathered barn, tilting to the side looked as if the March wind would blow it to the ground any minute. Oak and poplar trees swayed back and forth as the brisk wind blew its breath. The porch roof tilted to the side, in serious need of repair. She'd get it all fixed for him when she got the time, she promised herself.

Travis wagged his tail and whined for more affection. Indulging him, Johanna scratched behind his ear and ruffled his thick tan and white fur.

"I hope you like Florida, old boy," Johanna said, as the dog soaked in the attention. Though Smith loved the dog and talked to him constantly, he didn't waste time petting him.

Johanna glanced up as the screen door slammed and Smith returned with the key ring.

"When are you leaving?" she asked him, giving Travis a last pat before standing. She brushed dog fur off her jeans, which did little good, because Travis stuck his paws right back on her and leaned against her.

"Tomorrow morning." A rare smile tilted the side of his mouth. A light lit his eyes.

"So soon?" Johanna asked.

"Travis and I've been packed for a month now. Just waiting for you to come home. Gonna load up the truck tonight." He walked closer to her. "Now listen up," he said, his tone serious. "I've labeled all the keys with masking tape. This one," he said as he pointed to one key, "goes to the main entrance and this one is to the back door. Here's your cabin key.

The same one fits both the front and back door. The rest are in your office in the hotel.''

Pocketing the keys he'd handed to her, Johanna closed the distance between them, and hugged him. His reddish-tan skin tone darkened with age, bespoke his mixed Indian, African-American and Caucasian heritage. In back of her, Johanna could hear the rushing water from the Nottoway River, for which the town was named. It was the same river that rushed past her hotel, and hearing it was easier listening than any radio station could offer. Johanna squeezed her eyes shut tight, to keep the tears from seeping beneath her lids.

It was good to be home. Any problem that occurred, she'd deal with it.

Come hell or high water, she was opening her hotel on time. Her grand opening was scheduled for the third weekend in June. It was now March.

''I'll see you off tomorrow,'' she said to Smith. Turning, Johanna retraced her steps to her car before tears slid past her lids. Her security blanket and the man who made her ownership of the hotel possible was leaving the area. How could she ever thank him?

Johanna drove through a copse of budding trees up the two-lane, paved driveway to the Nottoway Inn. The budding of trees was a rebirth as much as her hotel was being reborn with all the improvements she'd lavished on it.

Johanna threw open the door of her red Ford Taurus and rushed out of the car to stand in the center of the drive for an unimpaired view. The Nottoway Inn stood in all its glory and melted into its surroundings as if had been there forever. For her, it had been.

Her breath hitched as she caught her first glimpse

of the bricked, art deco structure that had been built in the early nineteen hundreds.

The building stood forlorn in its unoccupied state. Its darkened windows beckoning visitors to bring out the life that had surrounded it in its glory in the twenties.

The change was staggering from its worn-down, neglected appearance of just a mere two months ago.

Johanna let her mind wander as she did when she was a child and envisioned the hotel blazing with chandeliers, vibrating with a cacophony of voices from inside.

She could almost hear its sigh as lovers strolled around the massive, majestic grounds hand in hand. The hotel and conference center would offer a sense of peace for harried business people taking a break from their daylong meetings, a refuge for those needing respite from their harried existence, a memorable starting point for honeymooners, memories for children who could run wild and explore nature along the countryside, and could tell their friends about the rides on hay-covered wagons.

This was all hers. And she had the papers to prove it. On shaky legs, Johanna took two steps toward the massive five-story, three-tiered setback building before she stopped on the cobblestoned circular drive.

In the yard, Patrick Stone, a local sculptor, had created a statue of Nottoway Indians around a campfire. A small waterfall in front of it gave the appearance of the group settling along the shoreline. The tribe had been torn apart more than a century ago, but traces of their heritage still lingered in some of the Nottoway residents.

The rush of water over the rock-inclined waterfall in back of the hotel sang out like music to the ears.

It was easily heard in the quiet, remote area. Johanna listened to the cadence for several minutes before rounding the building, taking the cobblestoned path strewn with flowers and shrubs, to the river. It only took a few moments standing on the bank before the sound and sight of the glistening water washed away the fatigue of the trip.

She faced the hotel. Most of the rooms had balconies where guests could enjoy the view from the privacy of their rooms. Two hundred yards to the right of the hotel stood a barn, almost hidden by the trees. When the flowers and trees were in full bloom, the structure would be completely hidden. Continuing her circle, Johanna faced the river again.

A gust of cool March wind shook the tree limbs and rippled the river's water. At this point, the river was almost three hundred feet wide, the widest spot in Nottoway. Hidden from view, a mile down on the opposite shore along twisting terrain was Karina Dye's restaurant. Johanna and Karina had been best friends since elementary school. Johanna couldn't wait to see her.

As the wind continued to blow, Johanna wished she'd worn a jacket.

Johanna hated to move away from the water, but there was so much to do. She could stay right where she was, enjoying the view for hours. By summer, her guests would be boating in these very waters.

Johanna's stomach growled, reminding her that she hadn't eaten since breakfast. Perhaps she'd pick up something simple for dinner at Tylan Chance's convenience center, then visit her parents first thing in the morning.

"Hello there. Are you lost in your dreams again?" a voice sounded in back of her making her jump. In the middle of nowhere, it just wasn't safe having strangers walk up on her. It was unsafe letting her mind wander to that extent.

Turning at the sound, Johanna immediately recognized the intruder. It was Jonathan Blake, Karina's brother—the man who she'd had a crush for as a child. Now, forty-one, a couple of gray strands peeped through the thick raven hair that she longed to touch. The gray didn't detract from his looks at all, Johanna thought, honing in on the mustache that edged his sensual lips.

"Of course," Johanna replied to his reference of her childhood penchant of lying on her stomach underneath the weeping willow tree in his yard, sharing her dreams with Karina. She tucked her hands in her pockets.

How long had she stood there? Glancing at the sky, she realized another hour and a half would pass before dark would completely descend upon them. Thick old trees shadowing the area made it seem later than it actually was. Perhaps that was why at six-one, with broad shoulders and a clean-shaven, sculptured face, Jonathan seemed larger than life—a forbidding character against the backdrop of the lonely Nottoway Inn. This man still had the power to send tiny flutters racing through her.

"Johanna? My God. You've . . . grown." She barely had time to take in the jeans and thick navy sweater where the sleeves were pushed up, revealing sinewy forearms dusted with black hairs, or pull her hands out her pockets before he reached out, grabbing her in his muscled arms and crushed her against his strong chest. The warmth of his chest seared into her breasts and exploded through her body, leaving her weak-kneed and breathless.

Johanna inhaled his masculine scent, which held a trace of cologne but more of his own clean, male essence. She wanted to stay there, snuggled close to him for hours.

With his hands on her shoulders, he stepped back to scan her from head to toe. His intimate glance sent licks of flames through her. Her body pulsed with sensations as though he'd touched her with his hands instead of his eyes. Shaking her head at her reaction, she sucked in a breath as he flicked her hair with the back with his fingers. Even that simple gesture sent pinpricks of awareness racing through her.

"What happened to the pigtails?" he finally asked in a voice so unlike its usual deep cadence. He sounded as if something was lodged in his throat.

Johanna hoped her own high-pitched laughter sounded normal. "You're the same old, dependable Jonathan."

Jonathan winced. Did she compliment him or insult him? The only thing he was certain of at that instant was that the five-foot-six woman standing before him had his heart pounding against his chest. The sensations from her breasts crushed against his chest spiraled out of control. How could this possibly be happening with his sister's best friend who was eight years younger than he?

Concentrating on her features, he tried to remember the little girl from years past. Her hair was a safe enough diversion, he thought. The naturally straight black tresses were an indication of her Indian heritage on her father's side of the family. She'd trimmed it to almost four inches down her back. Before she left, she'd either pinned it up or wore it in pigtails.

"Happy to be back now that your dreams have come true?" he asked her. "Who would have thought that you'd do such an extensive renovation or that the hotel would look so beautiful?"

"Very happy." She turned to face the water again, presenting Jonathan with a side view. "I've missed this place so." Her husky voice tilted Jonathan's equilibrium. The distance between them had stilled the raging fires, allowing him to take in her unique visage.

"Nottoway has that effect on people." Jonathan rocked back on his heels, continuing to watch Johanna instead of the water. How much she'd changed—how beautiful she looked in simple black jeans and a yellow T-shirt that outlined a perfectly rounded figure. As always, there was barely a speck of makeup, if any, on her face. That wholesome, natural appearance that suited her well had been enhanced. The willowy, stunning young creature with lustrous skin and luminous eyes had grown into a force to be reckoned with in the guise of a desirable woman.

And she thought of him as the same old, dependable Jonathan.

"I'm dying to see Karina," Johanna said.

"She can't wait to see you. She's working tonight." Then, before Jonathan knew what had hit him, he asked, "May I take you to dinner at her place?" After the words had slipped through his lips, he realized he was glad he'd asked.

Her uncertain glance skidded past him before she said, "Well . . ."

"As a welcome home," he interjected quickly. "You've got to eat sometime." He dug his hands in his pockets and held his ground as he awaited her reply.

"I'll need time to unpack the car and shower," she told him, looking toward her vehicle that was hidden by the massive hotel.

"I'll help you unpack." The idea of helping her shower held better merits. He wouldn't go there, though.

Her smile replaced the shadows created by the trees. "Now, that's an offer I can't refuse."

It didn't take long to unpack Johanna's few belongings into the renovated two-bedroom cedar cabin. The small structure contained a great room with a stone fireplace. The kitchen occupied one end of the room that led to a deck, which stretched only a few yards from the river.

Johanna's second bedroom was set up as an office, with a huge pine desk and a chair on rollers. The desk held a small hutch for a computer and Jonathan connected the computer for her while she showered.

After her shower, she donned navy silk evening slacks with a matching jacket.

"I have to call Mom before we leave," she warned Jonathan when she returned to the great room. "Someone is bound to see us at the restaurant and call her tonight."

Having had past experience with Gladys Jones, Jonathan could imagine the fireworks that would ensue. "Go ahead, I'll wait," he said from the office doorway. He went back to finish plugging the printer to the computer.

Hesitantly, Johanna sat on the couch and dialed her parents' home from the phone on the sofa table. On the second ring, her mother answered.

"Hello, Mom? I'm here," Johanna stated.

"Oh, that's wonderful. I'll get your dad to bring me right over." Her mother's cheery voice brought a warm smile to Johanna's face.

"Ah, Mom, I'll come by in the morning. I'm on my way out to eat."

"Well shucks. I just put a ham and a turkey in the oven for tomorrow. To celebrate. But I can whip up something real quick for you. Why didn't you tell me you were coming early?'' Gladys admonished.

"It was a last-minute decision. And I'll eat with you and Dad tomorrow.'' Johanna knew it wasn't going to be easy. It never was with her mother. "Don't worry though. I'm not going alone.''

"Well, who're you going with? Your dad and I want to see you.''

"I'm eager to see you, too, but Jonathan just happened to pass by as I was unpacking the car and offered to take me to dinner. I haven't had time to buy groceries yet.'' That was one more chore on her to-do list for tomorrow.

"Jonathan's there?'' The eagerness in her mother's voice gave her pause.

Johanna barely caught her groan at the slip. Why did she mention Jonathan's name? "Yes. He's taking me to Karina's restaurant.''

"Well, since it's Jonathan, it's all right. You know he's not dating anyone now. He hasn't since poor Sheryl died. Lord, bless her soul.'' Johanna imagined the wheels turning in her mother's head. Sheryl Newton had been Jonathan's fiancée.

She glanced at Jonathan, embarrassment spreading through her and then turned her back on him. "It's not a date, Mom,'' she all but whispered.

"You can make it into one,'' came Gladys' hopeful response.

Johanna sighed. "He's waiting for me. Tell Dad hello. I'll see you tomorrow.'' By tomorrow, her mother would have told everyone that Johanna was dating Jonathan.

"Have fun. And tell Jonathan I said hi.'' Johanna was completely exonerated for not visiting tonight.

"I will.'' She lowered the phone to the receiver.

Standing in the office door, Jonathan was actually grinning. "She got us engaged yet?" he joked.

"Give her until tomorrow, at least. She sends her regards." Johanna rubbed her forehead. "I don't know if this was a good idea or not. You know how Mom can blow things out of proportion."

"Come on. Don't worry about your mom." He took her jacket off the couch and held it for her to slip her arms inside.

"Easy for you to say," Johanna mumbled as she grabbed her purse.

She glanced at Jonathan out the corner of her eye. This was the first time she'd been anyplace with him without Karina . . . or a catastrophe. The last time she was alone with him was the night his fiancée died—the night before his wedding.

The Riverview restaurant was a ten-minute ride from the hotel, across the river and down the other bank. In spiked heels and a lovely off-white silk dress, Karina, her five-foot-four friend, was happily shocked to see her.

"Johanna!" Karina called out in a hushed but excited tone.

The women hugged.

"I'm so glad you're here," Karina said.

"And what about your brother?" Jonathan's deep voice intervened in their reunion.

"I always see you," Karina murmured as she turned back to Johanna. "How did you twist his arm into bringing you?"

"I never have to be coerced into eating with a beautiful woman," Jonathan said.

No wonder he was such a heartthrob Johanna

thought as heat stole over her. She hoped it didn't show.

"It's more like he's starved." Thankfully Karina seemed to miss the vibes flowing back and forth between the couple, and made light of the dinner.

"I hope you have a table with a view," Jonathan requested as another couple entered the restaurant.

"I do." Karina picked up menus, and passing a table that held a sculpture of a ship done by Patrick, she escorted them to the dining room.

The restaurant was packed with diners and a low buzz of conversation ensued. Johanna passed familiar faces as she followed Karina. Others must be new to the area. She immediately recognized catty Darlene Thompson, as they referred to her in high school, who never looked up, she was so engrossed in her conversation with a male companion.

Unfortunately, Karina stopped at a table next to Laura Miles and Jonathan held the chair for Johanna before he rounded the table to his own seat.

"The special tonight is fresh grilled trout, flown in today," Karina told them as she handed them menus.

"Sounds wonderful." Johanna loved fresh fish.

"It's delicious." Karina touched Johanna's arm. "We have to get together soon, Jo. I'll put together a small dinner party to introduce you to some friends. I'll call you."

"Sure. It'll be fun."

"Your waitress will be right with you." Karina turned and left, speaking to several of the diners on her way to the foyer. Johanna loved the warm atmosphere and Karina's attention to her guests.

When Johanna glanced up from her menu, she noticed several diners watching her table. "We're going to be the talk of Nottoway," she whispered to Jonathan over the menu.

"Doesn't bother me." Jonathan didn't bother to open his menu.

"Good evening. I'm Theresa," a young waitress with intricately braided hair said. "What can I get you to drink?"

Jonathan glanced at Johanna.

"I'll have iced tea," she told the woman.

"Make that two." Jonathan looked at the wine list. "Would you like white wine, Johanna?"

"A glass will be perfect."

"Two glasses of Chardonnay, please." After taking their drink orders, Theresa left.

"Have you decided on your meal yet?"

"I'll go with the special." She closed her menu and placed it by her napkin.

"I've never seen that hotel look so elegant," Jonathan said. "This is what it must have looked like in the early nineteen hundreds."

"I wanted it to be every bit as grand as it was back then. As a child I used to look at Smith's pictures of it for hours."

"To the disgust of your mother."

Johanna laughed. "She hated for me to spend so much time at the hotel. I nagged her to death about going there. I would make such a nuisance of myself, she'd let me go just to get some peace." Johanna sipped her water.

"And you always seemed so nice."

She set down her glass. "Not according to my mother. I was her most troublesome child." Even now Johanna remembered her mother's ringing tone. At the edge of her patience, she would throw her hands in the air and shriek.

"Must have been the middle-child syndrome."

"Or something." Johanna's mother never understood her drive or love for the Nottoway Inn. It was just . . . there.

"She's proud of you." Amusement flickered in the gaze that met hers. "You turned out okay."

"Why thank you, Mr. Blake." She loved his gentle camaraderie.

They glanced up as Theresa offered the wine to Jonathan to test. He sipped and nodded his approval. The waitress poured two glasses and placed Johanna's in front of her. Jonathan gave her their order and she left as quietly as she'd arrived.

An elegant older couple smiled up at them as Karina neared their table. Mr. and Mrs. Higabothum, owners of the Ice Cream Parlor, stopped long enough to speak a few words and welcome Johanna home before Mr. Higabothum ushered his wife, guiding her with a gnarled hand on her elbow to their table. "We do like to stop by every other week to dine. Nice to get out," Mrs. Higabothum said.

The familiar faces and country warmth was what Johanna missed most with her travels across the country as she'd managed a series of hotels.

Not five minutes had passed when Johanna heard a snappy remark.

"Bringing strangers to our town what with that new hotel," catty Darlene said. "Crime will rise. Watch and see." The pejorative statement came from in back of Johanna.

Johanna was on the verge of saying something when Jonathan reached across the table, resting his larger hand on hers. He squeezed, offering comfort.

"People will talk," he said, simply. "Most of the people in Nottoway welcome the improvements you've made. Any growing town needs a place closer than twenty-five miles for guests to stay. For once, I'll have accommodations for out-of-town businesspeople. I'm grateful I won't have to drive my clients all the way to Petersburg."

His tightening expression was replaced with a smile. "Look at the view."

She did, for the first time since sitting there. The sun had slid low, hanging in back of the trees and reflecting on the river. It lent a surreal orange glow. "It's beautiful," Johanna whispered.

"We don't get this view often."

"No. It's more common in Florida or the Midwest." Both of them watched as the sun slowly faded, the bitter remark soon forgotten.

Jonathan's warm hand remained on hers. Its warmth seeping through to her caused her to feel comforted, intimate and welcomed. Still, she'd known that everyone wouldn't welcome her back with open arms.

But even that peace was disturbed when Mr. and Mrs. Newton, Sheryl's parents, stopped at their table.

Jonathan stood and hugged Mrs. Newton and shook Mr. Newton's hand.

"How are you?" Jonathan asked. "You remember Johanna Jones, don't you?"

"Hello," Johanna smiled.

"We remember you. How are your folks?" Mrs. Newton asked her with a smile that didn't reach her eyes.

"They're fine, thank you."

Then she turned to Jonathan. "We're visiting Sheryl's grave tomorrow."

"Yes," Jonathan said. A year after Sheryl had died, he'd joined them when they made their yearly visit to the graveside, but he hadn't been back since. His heart wasn't in it. He had no love left for Sheryl.

"It's always hard on us. A parent never forgets,"

Mrs. Newton said, her eyes glassy. Her meaning that he had forgotten his fiancée was clear in her message.

"Come on honey, our table is ready. We'll be fine," Mr. Newton said to his wife.

"Well, enjoy your dinner," Jonathan said to them.

"Same to you." Mr. Newton escorted his wife to a table.

"Are you all right?" Johanna asked him as he settled in his chair.

"I'm fine." Tomorrow was the fourteenth anniversary of Sheryl's death.

The Newtons had unwittingly left a pall over the dinner.

CHAPTER 2

The sight of Johanna, standing by the river with the rushing water as a backdrop and the trees and birds serenading her, had taken Jonathan's breath away, and before he'd known what had hit him, he'd invited her to dinner.

Unable to sleep from thinking of her, he shifted positions, tangling his legs in the crisp, ironed sheets his housekeeper had changed earlier. Working from sunup to sundown, he never had problems falling asleep at night, so lying awake at 1:00 A.M., punching his pillow every five minutes was an unwelcome novelty.

Finally, giving up the fight, he rose from bed, catching his foot in the tangled mess. Freeing himself, he stretched his arms toward the ceiling, releasing the tension in his muscles, and rubbed his hands across his face. He used the illumination from the faint light filtering through the blinds to grab his jeans and a sweatshirt from a chair and slip them on.

Walking across the great room on the ground level of his old house, he pulled his jacket off the peg by the door, and unlatched the lock to amble out onto the bricked patio, trying to wash Johanna from his memory.

A full moon cast ghostly shadows on trees swaying in the wind and etched the perimeter of the yard. The March wind was brisk, cool, and invigorating.

Jonathan felt energized exactly when he actually wanted to feel sleepy.

Trying to blank Johanna from his mind in order to get a full night's sleep had been impossible. She was the first woman to awaken his senses since—he couldn't remember ever being this aware of a woman. Not even with Sheryl. He wondered whether the small voice of guilt still penetrated his conscience. She'd died in an accident the night before their wedding. He'd gotten the word of her death two hours after he'd told her he wouldn't marry her.

People thought he'd remained single all these years because he still grieved for her and was looking for another woman just like her. But that had been fourteen years ago.

The eve before their wedding, he'd found Sheryl in bed with another man, and that experience had dislodged the blinders from his eyes forever.

With one stroke, a woman could tear a man's heart into a million pieces. After so many years, her picture had dimmed. He barely remembered her features anymore, or what characteristics had drawn him to her in the first place. He even had trouble remembering the things they liked about each other. He still wondered whether the feelings had been real or coated by fresh youth dreaming at the mystery of romance. Perhaps the pretense was what he'd fallen in love with.

Soon after, he'd thrown himself into his business. His sister Karina's care had been his responsibility since he was twenty-two. Their parents had died in another accident, on a winding country road when Karina was fourteen.

Karina's care had taken enormous patience and time. He'd worried whether he was raising her the proper way. He worried over her slightest sniffles, about her boyfriends, whether she should even be out, but at the same time, he'd been loathe to stifle her spirit.

The final blow had come when she'd gotten pregnant in her senior year in college and married Victor Wallace, who wasn't the father of her children, without telling Jonathan. He blamed himself. That summer he shouldn't have left her with a housekeeper who'd been well into her sixties. But Karina had stayed in college without his supervision and she'd convinced him she'd be fine. She was responsible and she was twenty-one, after all.

And then she was bedridden for months because she was carrying triplets. Jonathan shook his head and smiled. Karina and her triplets had definitely kept him busy. But the marriage didn't last.

Now they had settled down with Phoenix Dye, the triplets' father and the man Karina loved. Jonathan had finally begun to relax. Karina's new husband took excellent care of her and their children. Jonathan had been relegated to the role of doting uncle.

Jonathan laughed. Since then, many mothers had thrown their daughters in his path, but he'd rather do without than settle for a woman who only wanted him for his money or because her mother determined him to be a "good catch."

Sheryl's mother had encouraged her to pursue him, but he'd believed Sheryl had truly loved him—that the decision was hers—until the night before their wedding.

Now he thought of Johanna who was the complete opposite of Sheryl. While Sheryl was a homebody and easily led, Johanna was definitely a career woman of the nineties and stubborn to a fault. She'd never marry a man because Gladys Jones wanted her to, or at least he hoped she wouldn't. She'd been away many years and he knew changes could occur over time. He only hoped she hadn't changed. Her fresh spirit had always intrigued him.

He, too, had changed over the years. He didn't need a woman at home waiting on him hand and foot any longer. Never did, actually.

Jonathan gazed into the star-filled night. He couldn't remember the last time he'd enjoyed himself as much as he had this evening. But Johanna was Karina's friend. Would she consider him a lecherous old man if he asked to take her out again? He winced. He'd be forty-one this year, pretty old for a thirty-three-year-old woman. But then again, she was thirty-three not fifteen.

And she pictured him as the same old Jonathan. Could she see him as a desirable man—a man who wanted her?

Jonathan often heard people whisper that he had everything. As the owner of a successful company, he had the weight of the town on his shoulders, while others slept peaceably, assured that Jonathan took the steps to ensure they stayed employed and would retire comfortably.

But he didn't have everything. He went home to an empty house, a solitary meal with only himself for company. He slept in his king-sized bed—alone.

Until now, the thought of a different pattern had eluded him. Through the years, he'd had discrete alliances—out of town—away from the gossipers. His last affair ended a year ago.

Seeing Johanna today had driven him to desire more. He wanted her here with him.

Jonathan sighed, turned and walked across the bricked patio. Entering the house, he clicked the lock in place behind him. Sleep still eluded him, but he had a big meeting tomorrow. He had to at least try to get some sleep.

The more crucial question that came to mind was whether he'd be willing or ready to pursue anything with Johanna, knowing Gladys Jones would interfere every step of the way.

That woman could annoy the heck out of the most patient saint. And Jonathan was no saint.

"Knock, knock," Johanna said through the screen door. Opening it, she entered her mother's familiar small kitchen, which smelled of eggs, bacon and homemade biscuits.

She barely had time to glimpse the pink housedress her mother wore or the yellow and beige café curtains hanging from the windows before she heard her mother's cheerful voice emerge from near the stove.

"Oh, my stars!" Gladys Jones ran over to hug her daughter, enveloping her in big, warm arms. She leaned back, tears streaming down her plump cheeks as she held on to her middle child.

"Lordy, aren't you a sight for sore eyes?" Henry Jones, her dad, who was leaning over to get something out the cabinet, stood and ambled over. He patted her on the shoulders as Gladys held on for dear life. He looked comfortable in his red checked flannel shirt and worn jeans.

Gladys rocked her back and forth for several seconds before she let Johanna go to hug her dad. He had gray peppered throughout his hair and her mom had the occasional gray strand. Johanna never thought of her parents as getting old. Fifty-eight didn't seem old at all. At that moment, Johanna realized she'd stayed away from home much too long.

"I sure am proud of you, girl," her dad began. "That hotel is a beaut," he said as he leaned back under the cabinet and pulled out a bag labeled "birdseeds." "I drive by there every day on my way home."

"Everybody's talking about that hotel. Never seen it look so good," her mom exclaimed, dabbing at her eyes with a tissue. "Your dad took me by there the other day." She went back to scrambling eggs on the stove.

"Thanks," Johanna said, slightly embarrassed even though it was comforting to be back home and have the approval of those she loved.

"I have to run to town and pick up some grass seeds." Her dad approached her and hugged her again. "Visit with your mother for a while. She's been cooking up a storm all week," her dad said as he let her go.

Johanna turned to her mom. "You didn't."

"I just cooked up a little something. Just your favorites: ham, turkey, fried chicken, macaroni and cheese, collard greens, string beans, potato salad, candied yams and lemon chess pie. Your favorites is all." She was clearly proud of her feast. "We're going to have a celebration."

"Mom, that's enough food for an army. Who's going to eat it all?"

"It's just a family affair. Your brother and sister and her family are coming. I just thought it'd be nice to have my family around me for a night."

"Oh, Mom. You didn't have to do all that work.

You're probably sore all over." Johanna hugged her mom again and led her to a chair.

"Now, now." She patted Johanna's back. "I got my whole family right here. I couldn't be happier." She took a tissue and dabbed at her eyes again. "Now, tell me about Jonathan while I fix your breakfast." She started to get up again, but Johanna stayed her move.

Johanna glanced at the stove heaping with food. "You sit and talk to me while I fix my plate. Have you eaten yet?" she asked her.

"I ate hours ago. I'm waiting for you to tell me about Jonathan."

Johanna went to the walnut cabinet and pulled it open to take one of the blue and white plates out, the same plates she'd used as a child. "Nothing to tell, really. We just met at the river when I was looking over the place. He took me to dinner for a welcome home. That's all." Johanna dished up eggs, two slices of bacon and a biscuit, glancing at her mom who sat on the edge of the seat, enraptured in the tale. Keeping the tale simple might keep her mother from telling everyone they were getting married by the end of the night.

"That's all?" her mom asked, disappointment clouding her voice.

"That's all," Johanna repeated. She needed to downplay it so her mom wouldn't escalate it into something embarrassing. "You know how I was always underfoot with Karina in high school. He was always taking us someplace." Johanna bit into a fluffy, buttered biscuit without thinking about calories or fat grams for a change.

"You could make it into something." Standing, Gladys went to the silverware drawer, snapping it open in irritation. Grabbing a fork, she handed the utensil to her daughter.

"No, I can't. And don't you make anything more out of it. Don't go around saying anything to embarrass me." Sometimes her mom didn't take the hint and you had to come right out and tell her.

Gladys leveled a motherly glare on her daughter. "I'm your mother, Johanna. I wouldn't embarrass you." Affronted, she padded to the stove, grasped the empty frying pan, dropped it into the dishwater and put her disappointment into vigorously scrubbing the pan.

"I'm sorry," Johanna said. "It's just that in small towns, people talk."

Gladys glanced at Johanna over her shoulder. "I've lived here all my life. You think I don't know?" She went back to scrubbing dishes.

Johanna had only been in the house for five minutes, and already she'd disappointed her mother. Similar visions of her childhood held much of the same. It wouldn't do to tell her mom that she was one of the worst culprits. "Of course you do." Johanna sat at the table and dug into the best breakfast she'd had since leaving home. A sense of disappointment suddenly surrounded her. She'd seen Smith off earlier that morning, and now she was arguing with her mom.

Jonathan remained at the head of the table in the main conference room at Blake Industries while he patiently waited for everyone except James Evans, his company's new vice president, to file out.

From the opposite end of the table, James rose from his chair, strode to the sideboard and picked up the silver coffeepot to top off his coffee. He raised an eyebrow at Jonathan who shook his head no. On his return to his seat, James closed the door. Snatching up his folder, he moved to a chair closer to Jonathan.

The meeting had covered their bid for a major contract for the largest airline in Singapore. Jonathan wanted the Asian business so badly he could taste it.

Tall and formidable, James was energetic, pragmatic, and he knew the Asian market. Best of all, he knew how to sell to and court clients, which was why Jonathan brought him aboard and why, for the first time, he was letting someone else fly out to take care of that side of the business instead of doing it himself.

It was time he delegated more higher level duties. But he'd almost had to glue himself to the oak chair to allow James to do it.

Work had controlled his life for far too long.

"What are you going to do about the merger offer from Tri-Parts, Inc.," James asked him.

Tri-Parts was a small airplane parts company that wanted to merge with Blake Industries, Jonathan's company. He sensed the tension in the other man.

"I'm not interested in a merger. A merger would necessitate giving up some control," Jonathan told him and watched him slowly relax. "Some employees would probably have to be laid off. Our business is growing and I don't plan any layoffs in Nottoway. Blake Industries is the lifeblood of the town. I intend to keep it that way." Jonathan picked up his pen to make a note on a leather-bound pad. "Draft a refusal letter to them," he said to James before he turned the discussion to the Singapore airline. They had three months to finalize their bid.

James nodded his head and scribbled notes on his own pad. "Will do."

Jonathan imagined the younger man's concern for

his own new position, which could easily change in a merger. Married to Johanna's older sister, Pamela, James had moved his family to Nottoway four months ago and purchased a lovely new home.

The intercom buzzed, interrupting them. Rising from his chair, in two quick strides, he reached over and punched the intercom button. "Barbara, hold all my calls, please." Barbara Dicks had been his secretary since he started the company eighteen years ago, and she knew him well. It surprised him that she'd interrupted a meeting.

"Jonathan, Gladys Jones is extremely insistent." Caution laced her voice.

"I'll take it." Puzzled at why Gladys would call him when she'd never called before, he depressed the blinking phone button, and leaned against the credenza.

"Hello, Mrs. Jones. How are you?"

"I'm fine, thank you, Jonathan. I know you're at work so I don't want to keep you," she rushed out the words in a hesitant voice.

He glanced at his watch. "That's quite all right."

"Well, I'm throwing a little something together for Johanna tonight. I remember how kind you were to her as a child, and I thought I'd just invite you over, too. I've cooked up a storm for it."

Jonathan mentally ran through his schedule. "I'll be happy to come. What time?" he asked her.

"Well, we're actually having dinner here, so don't eat before you come. How does six sound? Do you think you can get away from work by then?"

"Sounds good. I'll see you at six tonight." Jonathan disconnected, knowing he'd opened a can of worms with that one dinner.

"I'm surprised she invited you," James said of his mother-in-law. "She was adamant about having only family there. She must consider you one of the family," James grinned. "Welcome aboard."

Jonathan couldn't muster up a smile. He was leery of another mother pushing her daughter toward him. But there was something about Johanna that fascinated him and made it impossible for him to refuse. He'd have to trust that she was as honest now as she'd been before she left.

The temperature had dropped by the time Johanna left the house. She wore emerald green slacks and a white sweater with a huge green leaf on the shoulder.

The table, laden with food, created the mouth-watering aromas that layered the air when she entered the kitchen promptly at six.

Johanna was surprised to see Jonathan standing in the kitchen with her mother who entertained him with family tales while she thrust barbecued wingettes and other hors d'oeuvres onto a plate and handing it to him.

A familiar shiver of awareness rippled through Johanna and she tried not to let her attraction show. She glanced at the pleased expression on her mom's face.

Johanna could just die right on the spot, imagining what her mom could have said to Jonathan to get him to the family dinner. And he acquiesced under her pressure like putty in a child's hands.

"Hi," he said, as he lifted a wingette to his mouth and took a bite.

"Hello," she mumbled cautiously, wondering if he could read her thoughts.

"Hi, darling," Gladys, full of cheer, greeted her daughter. "Look who just happened to drop by. I told him he may as well stay for dinner. I certainly have enough food cooked up to seat an extra guest."

A quick look at Jonathan had him grinning. "Wasn't that kind of your mother? I didn't know what I was going to eat for dinner tonight."

Gladys patted his hand. "You're welcome here anytime, dear. You know that."

Johanna shook her head. She'd warned Jonathan. "I'll wash my hands and help you get the food on the table," Johanna told her mom.

"No, no. Pam can help me when she gets here. Go on in the living room and keep Jonathan company." Shoving another plate of hors d'oeuvres in Johanna's hand, she shooed them out of the kitchen with a dish towel. Subtlety wasn't a word one would associate with Gladys.

"How was your first day back?" Jonathan asked as they sat on Gladys' plastic covered sky-blue couch that looked as new as it did the day she'd purchased it.

Pictures of the family in elaborate frames covered the tabletops. Several photos had been blown up and hung from the wall, along with a picture of Jesus some door to door salesman had talked her mom into buying years ago.

"Busy. The day started with arguing for hours on the phone to get my drapery here on schedule."

Jonathan could imagine her fighting to the end. "It'll get better."

"One day," Johanna agreed. "What did Mom tell you to get you here?"

"She invited me to dinner. I'm glad she did. I was starving. And I wanted to see you again."

That statement ignited a fire in Johanna and her perusal of him assured her that he did look pleased to be here—with her. "Well, if it's okay with you.

She'll have you here every weekend until you marry me."

"If nothing else, I'll be well-fed. Think I'll get fat from her cooking?"

Looking at his trim form, his washboard stomach, Johanna raised an eyebrow. "Are you fishing for compliments?"

"Are any forthcoming?" His tone lowered to a seductive level that had an immediate effect. Johanna's heartbeat skidded into overdrive. But hearing her mother's raised voice when she greeted her grandchildren offered a convenient reprieve from his seduction. She released a breath.

Pamela Evans had four children. Nicole was the oldest at fifteen, Monica was twelve, Anthony eight and Trevor, the youngest, was going through his terrible-two stage.

"Will you excuse me a moment?" she said to Jonathan. "I haven't seen the children in a month."

"Of course."

Johanna stood, escaped through the dining room to the kitchen and amid "Aunt Johanna" greetings, she hugged them all and hefted Trevor on her hip. He stayed there for less than two minutes. "I think you've all grown at least two inches," Johanna said to them. They seemed to change so rapidly.

"You're teasing us," Nicole said, looking all grown up.

"I'm just so happy to see you."

James and Pamela entered the house, James sporting an amused smile. Something was up, Johanna thought suspicious of that look.

"What a surprise to see you here, Jonathan," James joked and looked at Gladys.

Jonathan merely laughed at the man's foolishness.

"Hello, everyone," Pamela said.

James glanced at Gladys whose innocuous demeanor could fool the most dubious observer as she bustled about. "How's my favorite mother-in-law?" James asked, and wrapped his arms around Gladys' ample girth. They'd always gotten along famously.

"I'm your only mother-in-law," she told him. "How is my favorite son-in-law?" she asked returning his warm greeting.

"Ready to stuff myself." He rubbed his trim stomach as he always did and Gladys always outdid herself to present pleasing dinners for him.

"Pam, help me take the food into the dining room. As soon as that son of mine . . . "

"I haven't seen the house this full since Christmas," Emmanuel said, slamming the door behind him.

"Well, it's about time, baby," Gladys said for once not cautioning him for slamming the door.

Emmanuel rolled his eyes. His mom would forever think of him as the baby of the family even though he stood eight inches taller than she. He took his baseball cap off his bald head and threw the cap on the peg by the kitchen door. It swung back and forth but didn't fall.

Henry entered after his son and everyone helped carry the food to the table. Gladys maneuvered the seating so that Jonathan and Johanna could sit next to each other in the dining room. Even the children's screams that they wanted to be next to their aunt didn't win out over Gladys' determination to do everything in her power to get the matchmaking moving in the proper direction.

Johanna was so embarrassed by her mother's blatant attempts that it took a while for her to enjoy her food, even though everyone else attacked theirs with gusto.

"You getting more time to yourself now that you've hired James as vice president?" Gladys asked Johnathan during a lull in conversation. She watched Trevor gnaw to the bone the chicken leg that she'd handed him earlier. The tasty leg was enough to keep him quiet for a spell.

Jonathan swallowed his food. "Yes, I do. James is a wonderful addition to the company."

"Heard you're spreading to Asia," Henry said lifting the bowl of candied yams and dishing a spoonful on his plate. "You're really expanding."

"We're trying." Jonathan hoped to get the turkey into his mouth before it cooled.

"When are you going to marry Aunt Johanna?" Anthony asked, reaching for the candied yam bowl his grandfather had just discarded.

Everyone stopped eating. Silence hovered with the utensils in the air.

"She hasn't asked me yet," Jonathan answered smoothly in the lull.

Gladys came out of her trance. "Hush up and eat your food, young man," she admonished.

"But, Grandma, you said . . . "

"Hush up, I said, and clean your plate."

Jonathan's mouth twitched with amusement as everyone focused on Gladys, who busied herself putting a heaping spoonful of candied yams on the boy's plate. She'd previously told him he couldn't have any until after he finished his dinner.

"Mr. Blake," Monica said, "aren't you supposed to ask Aunt Johanna to marry you?"

"Children are to be seen not heard at the dinner table," Gladys sputtered.

But Jonathan took it all in stride as he glanced at Johanna. She stiffened and stains of color appeared on her cheeks. "It's a new day now that we're nearing the twenty-first century. Women can do anything a man can do, which means she can ask me to marry her, can't you Jo." He used the nickname that only he and Karina used years ago.

"Are you going to ask him?" Anthony asked around a mouth of candied yams, vegetables and meat forgotten. "I hope a girl doesn't ask me." He swallowed and made gagging sounds at the thought.

"No, I'm not." She glared in her mother's direction. Where else could they have heard mumbling about marriage? Johanna didn't have the excuse to faint from a tight corset women wore in past centuries. Her only recourse was for her heart to pound and warmth to spread across her face.

"Stop talking and eat your food," Gladys snapped at her grandchildren.

"But, Grandma," Anthony started again. "At home, we always talk . . . "

"Go to the basement and play with your toys, right now!" she told him as she busied herself with piling more candied yams on his plate.

"But, I'm still hungry. I didn't get any cake yet," he whined.

"And you're not going to if you keep talking," Gladys glared at him.

"You sure are grumpy tonight," he muttered.

"Anthony?" his father's warning had the effect Gladys' mumbling didn't, and it was several minutes late by Johanna's reasoning.

James turned the course of the conversation. It was minutes before Johanna completely relaxed.

At the end of the meal, everyone was so stuffed they could hardly move. If every person didn't stuff themselves, Gladys' feelings were hurt.

Friday night, Johanna knew she was in high heaven, but the discussion about marriage still stung. Johanna would bet several hard-earned dollars that her mother had talked about her wish to get Johanna married off to Jonathan around the children.

Johanna's final embarrassing episode occurred when she was ready to leave.

"Johanna, I tell you it's just so dangerous for young ladies to go home alone nowadays. Jonathan, would you mind following her and see to it that she gets inside all right?" Gladys patted him on the arm.

Emmanuel looked at his mom. "I'll be glad . . . ouch," he said as Gladys jabbed him in the arm with a fork.

"I'll be happy to see her home safely," Jonathan gallantly offered, struggling not to laugh.

"Mom, I've been seeing myself home for years," Johanna snapped, discomfiture quickly turning to annoyance.

"Still, you're in the middle of nowhere. I'll sleep a lot better if you weren't alone."

"I'll call you from home. There's no need for Jonathan to escort me to my door. I've got security on duty at the hotel at night."

"I have to pass the hotel anyway," Jonathan interrupted smoothly. "Thank you for a delicious dinner, Mrs. Jones." He smiled at the woman.

"You're welcome, dear. Don't be a stranger, now." Gladys was in seventh heaven now that she'd gotten her way.

Jonathan's headlights followed Johanna all the way home. He parked beside her car and exited his mint-green Infiniti.

"I'm so sorry you had to drive out of your way," Johanna apologized.

"Don't worry yourself so."

Johanna was surprised when he'd shut the car door and followed her into her cabin.

"Would you like to come in for coffee or . . . something?" she asked still smarting by her mother's very obvious matchmaking tactics.

"Coffee would be fine." The something would be even better, Jonathan thought, but he'd settle for coffee, he thought as he watched her hips sway as she walked in front of him.

Her cottage was the farthest one from the hotel. Johnna had unpacked and the place already looked lived in. Built-in half-height bookcases, already filled with books, stood along one wall.

"It didn't take you long to move in," he said glancing around.

"I didn't have much. In hotel management, I traveled a lot and didn't see the sense in accumulating things I'd have to get rid of later. Have a seat while I put the coffee on."

Instead, Jonathan wandered into the small kitchen area with her. He liked watching her move around. She put a lot of energy into everything she did. It wasn't long before she backed into him.

"Oops." She turned toward him. Only a foot of space separated them. "I thought you were in the living room." Her soft, sweet voice went to his head like a strong wine.

"The view's better in here," he whispered just before he closed the distance between them, leaned toward her and captured her lips with his own. For a moment she merely stood there, then slowly she responded to his touch. Only then did he put his arms around her and draw her body against his long, hard frame. He'd waited all night for this.

He sighed before he deepened the kiss. And while

he enjoyed the taste of her, he felt her hands on his back. Just maybe she felt some stirring for him—the attraction wasn't one-sided, he thought as he lost himself in her essence.

He was astounded by his body's reaction to her. Reaching a hand underneath the soft sweater, he felt her skin, smooth, warm and soft.

He was burning up with desire.

"You feel it, too, don't you?" His lips parted from hers long enough to whisper against her face. His hardness pressed against his trousers in reaction to her softness pressing against him. But it was too soon. Much too soon for the release he craved with her and only her.

She nodded.

He bent his head again to taste her, knowing he wouldn't get his fill tonight, but craving the teasing anyway. Just one more kiss.

"Let me take you out tomorrow night." He swirled his tongue along her delicate lobe.

She inhaled sharply. "Are you sure this is what you want?" she asked, her delicate, insistent fingers scoring his back.

"Absolutely positive," he whispered, drawing her closer to his body.

"The talk . . . "

"Let them," he murmured, and kissed her again—deeper, harder. "Talk never bothered you before."

"Still doesn't. You have a reputation to uphold," she reminded him.

"I don't think I like this reputation you're imposing on me. But I've got to leave." Distance was better for now. The electricity between them was new and powerful. This time, Jonathan would take his time to discover where these emotions would lead. He wouldn't run away from them, but neither would he indulge himself until he was certain of both their feelings.

By the time the coffee was ready, Jonathan had closed the cabin door and headed to his car.

CHAPTER 3

Johanna stopped by Patrick Stone's house on Saturday morning. Several statues were in his yard and on his porch. He used an old, weather-beaten barn located fifty yards from the back door of his house as his studio.

A month ago, he'd told Johanna that he'd used some of the salary she'd paid him to renovate the barn so that he could use it for work year-around. An old wood heater had been added.

Johanna had commissioned him to sculpt for her full time a year ago. He'd finished the last of the projects last week, the biggest being the sculpture displayed in front of the hotel. Before that, Patrick had given small pieces away as gifts. When the company he worked for moved farther south, he created pieces to be sold at Karina's restaurant, local fairs and flea markets. Now, a gallery in Petersburg showcased his work, but still he hadn't been making enough money to live completely off his art. That circumstance changed a year ago.

He'd jumped at the opportunity to sculpt full time when Johanna had approached him. Having his work displayed at the hotel would give him more exposure.

Wearing a thick sweater and drinking what she assumed was coffee, he sat on the creaky porch swing, using his foot on the floorboard to push the swing back and forth. Johanna loved that old swing. Huge porches and swings were features of the south she loved most.

"Johanna," he said, standing as she approached the steps, "it's so good to see you."

"Patrick, your work is breathtaking." She closed her eyes. It was so difficult to describe what she felt about his sculptures. "I stared at that statue so long when I arrived. Thank you for a tremendous job," she told him and climbed the porch steps.

Patrick worked his mouth a few times and plopped into the seat before a croak emerged. "Thanks," he whispered, "I was so worried."

"Worried! About what? You've created some wonderful masterpieces at the hotel."

Then he was all motion, tearing the napkin from under his cup and dabbing at his eyes. "You just don't know," he whispered. He was just like his sentimental father when the older man had imbibed too much.

"I know," she said. She knew what it was to dream. Anybody who'd ever desired something so badly they could taste it would understand.

"Are you working on other pieces now that you've finished this project?"

"Sure am." He sniffed and nodded. "Come on. Let me give you a tour of my studio." He grabbed her hand and they headed out back. Grabbing a key out of his pocket, he opened one of the huge double barn doors.

Johanna scanned the enormous one-room structure. Tables, pedestals and the floor were littered with sculptures. Her attention focused on one in particular. "Is that a likeness of Mrs. Drucilla and Luke?"

He nodded. "I watched them embracing one day when I visited Tylan. It happened so quickly, you know. The light just caught them a certain way that day." He walked over to the sculpture and touched it. His touch was like a caress. "The image wouldn't leave my mind," he said, glancing at Johanna. "I had to create an image of that scene that would last forever. They're such good people," he finished.

"That they are." Johanna nodded. The older couple weren't fanciful. They were plain old people who spoke little but were always available to extend a helping hand or dispense valuable advice when needed. They were the rock of the town.

"Patrick," Johanna whispered at a loss of words as she continued to scan the room filled with rich treasures. The room needed to be padlocked and the treasures needed to be placed in a museum or a gallery for all to see.

Most of the pieces depicted days gone by, snapshots of rural life that would never be seen again. They were likenesses of many scenes Johanna had witnessed as a child, while growing up in the country.

The sculptures of horses swimming in the Nottoway, legs frozen in a kick beneath the waters, seemed so lifelike. There was one of a little girl reading beneath the pecan tree. Johanna marveled at farm scenes of an old man plowing his field of cotton on his John Deere tractor, a deer drinking out of a spring, a barnyard full of animals—chickens, cows, pigs—a man guiding a plow being pulled by a mule, kids dropping sweet potato slips and using a stick to secure them in the ground, a harvesting scene of hauling bushel baskets on a wagon down a row of sweet potatoes.

Water scenes included a man fishing from a pond, a man wearing hip boots fishing several feet out in the river, kids jumping in the river, kids swimming in the river, an old woman boating in the Nottoway, a woman washing clothes on a washboard at the river. One even depicted a baptizing at the river.

An old country store with a sign advertising ten ginger snap cookies for a penny, ballerinas, and assorted individual animals were also featured. He'd even sculpted one of Smith's old pictures of Louis Armstrong playing in the lobby of the Nottoway Inn.

"I want to buy that one," Johanna said.

"It's yours," he said.

Before she left, they haggled out a price for the piece she was buying. The only problem was that he was trying to charge too little for his creations.

Several months ago, Johanna had hired Pam, her sister, as director of sales for the hotel. Pam had worked in that position for several years at a resort until she became pregnant with her third child. At that point, she quit her job to become a full-time mom.

Pam was ready to work outside the home again on a part-time basis, but she agreed to work full time until the grand opening in June and she had the opportunity to train an assistant. Then, she planned to cut back on her hours.

Now, Johanna and Pam read through job applications in the sales office. The managers—housekeeping, front office, restaurant—had been hired months ago along with their staffs. The task hadn't been difficult since many workers who'd been driving twenty-five and fifty miles to Petersburg and Richmond looked forward to working closer to home.

In two weeks, the hotel would open and they still didn't have an assistant sales manager. Not all of the interior work was completed, but the rooms and lobby area were almost done. Johanna couldn't afford to wait any longer.

Jonathan had businessmen coming to town, and he had booked rooms for them. Conventions were scheduled, weekend packages already paid for.

Even now the gardeners were planting shrubbery, azaleas and countless other springtime flowers, adding splashes of color to the landscape.

With the windows open, Johanna inhaled the sweet smell of earth, greenery and clear, crisp country air.

"Karina told me someone was asking questions about the hotel last night in her restaurant, like who the owner was," Pam said during a lull.

Johanna looked up from the application she was reading. "I thought everyone in Nottoway knew."

"They do, but he wasn't local. He wore an expensive Italian suit, sort of stood out from everyone else. She thought he might be interested in buying the hotel."

That immediately caught Johanna's attention. "It's not for sale and won't be in my lifetime." Johanna wondered why the man hadn't approached her.

Pam held up her hands. "You don't have to convince me. Everything you've done since you were seven has been focused on owning this hotel. You were a fanatic about earning money, and you saved every cent." She chuckled. "I remember that piggy bank you'd put every penny in. I spent my money on dolls, doll clothes and play makeup." Pam smiled at her sister sitting across the desk from her. "I'm so happy for you."

"I can barely stand on the ground I'm so happy, Pam. But," she said, tapping an application, "I'm not there yet." Once the grand opening occurred, Johanna would feel as if she'd crossed a hurdle. But until then, there was so much work to do and still so many decisions left to be made.

"Close enough. And you deserve it."

"Thanks," she said, glancing at the application. "This application looks interesting. This woman has worked in sales in a hotel in Richmond for four years." Johanna finished reading the application and handed the pages across the desk to her sister.

While Pam scanned the contents, Johanna thought about her childhood. Standing on a wooden crate Smith had made for her so that she could see out from behind the desk, she'd been seven when she waited on her first customer by herself. Wearing his fishing hat and vest, Smith watched a few minutes then asked the housekeeper to keep an eye on her. The woman had barely nodded her head when he eagerly left for his favorite pastime, fishing on the Nottoway.

"Second door to the right," Johanna's secretary, Nancy Hill's voice sounded from down the hallway, cutting into her memories. Johanna glanced at the door.

A few seconds later, a man, wearing a brown shirt with a floral motif patch across the pocket silently came into view, carrying a huge vase of roses in his hand.

"My goodness!" Pamela exclaimed.

"I'm looking for Johanna Jones," he said, peering at papers on the clipboard in his other hand.

"I'm Johanna." Standing behind Pamela's desk,

she quickly rounded it, taking the vase he extended to her. The arrangement was much heavier than it appeared. "Thank you." She inhaled the pleasant odor wafting from the roses and couldn't stifle a smile as she shuffled papers aside on the desk to make room for the vase.

The man took a pen out his shirt pocket. "Sign here, please."

With one last sniff, Johanna signed the paper with only half her attention.

"I wonder who they're from?" Pamela asked, searching for a card.

Johanna realized her purse was in her own office. "Pam, do you have something to tip him with?"

"Sure." Severing her attention from the flowers, she rounded the desk, pulled her purse out of the bottom drawer, dug into the wallet for some bills and handed them over. After she'd stuffed the purse back into the drawer and closed it, she resumed her search for the card.

"Thank you." The florist nodded, turned and left while scribbling on his clipboard.

"Don't let me forget to pay you back," Johanna said, reaching for the card herself.

"Who are they from? Somebody must be missing you from Washington." Pamela leaned over and inhaled. Then she turned sideways, attempting to read the card.

Johanna remembered the last time she'd received roses. They were from Jonathan after her senior graduation, thanking her for being a great friend to Karina. Then, he'd given her six, not two dozen. Johanna wanted to savor the moment. She smelled them as she tore the flap on the envelope, their aroma throwing off their delicious scent and warming her heart.

"Well?" Pam asked, impatiently reaching out for the small card.

Johanna slapped her hand back. She took the card out of the envelope and read. It simply said, "Welcome home," signed with Jonathan.

"Uh oh," Pam said.

"They're from Jonathan."

Pam raised an eyebrow. "After just one night? Girl, what did you do to that man?"

"It wasn't like that," Johanna assured Pam, if not herself. "He's being kind." But the memory of his electric touch the night of the dinner sprang to Johanna's mind, landed right in her stomach and settled there.

"Kind." Pam leaned across the desk and tapped a finger against the vase. "If I wasn't a happily married woman, I'd take the two dozen *kind* any day."

It took a few moments to divert her attention from the roses. More for her benefit than Pam's, Johanna finally said, "Let's get back to business," and tried unsuccessfully to keep her mind on target. How on earth was she going to think of sales applications when Jonathan had claimed her mind? Was that his intent?

"Jonathan, Johanna Jones on line one," came Barbara's crisp voice on the intercom later that day.

Jonathan picked up, delighted to take a break from business projections to speak to her.

"The roses are absolutely gorgeous. I would say you shouldn't have, but I'm enjoying them too much. Thank you," she whispered softly.

Why was pleasure sluicing through her at hearing his voice? She was losing her mind.

"You're welcome."

"You couldn't have given me a better welcome present, but I thought the dinner was my welcome gift," she said, still relishing his deep, mystical voice.

"There's no law against more than one gift, is there? I'm glad you're pleased. But," he said, "there's something you can do to please me." The pitch of his voice lowered.

"What is it?" Johanna asked, pleasure dancing through her while she admonished herself to calm down. This was Jonathan, for goodness' sake, the solid rock. He wasn't a swash-buckling hero.

"You can have dinner with me tonight—at Karina's," he told her.

"Are you sure you want this? Every tongue in town will wag at seeing us together twice." Johanna wasn't really worried but Jonathan was always a private person.

"Let them," he said with a definite finality.

Johanna waited several heartbeats. "What time?" she asked, pleased that he wanted to be with her as much as she wanted to be with him.

"I've got a meeting at three. Seven okay?"

"Seven it is."

Jonathan hung up, an unexplainable lightness in his mood. He vowed to keep the meeting short and to the point. It wasn't often that he had something to look forward to in the evening. He was definitely looking forward to sitting across the table from Johanna again, catching a whiff of her subtle perfume. He could almost feel her soft hands on his back. Shifting in his seat, Jonathan glanced at his watch.

Perhaps he could move the meeting to tomorrow, he thought, reaching for the phone when a quick knock preceded the opening door. James came through, wearing a grave expression.

"Jonathan. We just got word that a plane made an emergency landing shortly after take off at O'Hare. It seems the delta bypass indicator flashed."

"What caused it?"

"The problem was the engine filter, and the serial number indicated it was one of ours. They said it's happened three times within the last two days."

"Did a bad shipment go out?" he asked. "Get word to engineering right now, and have the equipment and every filter checked before it leaves here."

"I've already done that."

"What the hell is going on? What happened to quality control?"

Standing, Jonathan grabbed his jacket from the back of his chair. "We triple-check those parts to make sure they aren't defective. We can't send out defective parts and stay in business. In this business, people's lives are at stake and I won't have it!" Icy anger coursed through him.

He punched the intercom with his index finger. "Barbara, get Ronald Newton in here right now," he told her and disconnected.

"Jonathan." That single word from James stopped him in his tracks. "You hired me to take care of this division. That means you let me handle it."

"We can't afford to lose contracts," Jonathan snapped. "We're trying to expand and we can't expand if we're sending out defective parts."

James stood his ground as he looked unflinchingly at Jonathan. "I know you've handled all the problems in the past, which is why you haven't had time for a life outside of work. But now, you've hired me to take some of the pressure off of you. I can't do my job thoroughly if you're going to do it for me," he said and neared the desk. "I'm good at what I do. I'm not new at handling these problems. Just let me do my job, Jonathan.''

Jonathan slowed. Everything James said was true. He had hired him to handle this, but when trouble came, Jonathan had always handled it, had always been on top of it. Was he ready and willing to loosen his control?

Jonathan took just a few seconds to make a decision and prayed it was the right one. "We're talking about the survival of the Aerospace parts division. That's fifty percent of the company.''

"I realize that. It doesn't change the facts.''

Slowly, Jonathan dropped into his seat. "All right. I'm leaving it in your hands. You had better be aware of the full implications of your decisions.''

"I am.'' James turned and strode to the door. With his hand on the doorknob, he stopped and turned. "I'll keep you abreast of what's happening.'' Opening the door, he exited the room, closing the door quietly and quickly behind him.

Jonathan heard him mumbling something to Barbara out front.

Running a hand across his head, Jonathan's face tightened with tension. He swiveled his soft leather burgundy seat to face the window.

Instead of a view of the forest as many executives would want, his view focused on the heartbeat of the main courtyard, looking out on the factory and the main hub of his company. Even now, he spotted a driver in a safety hat steering a forklift across a paved lot.

Faulty parts. Every employee knew how crucial each part they made was to the survival of the business, to the progress of the town and to the safety of the aircraft those parts went into.

The arms of Blake Industries extended to the whole

town. It paid for school and recreational facilities alike.

He remembered that his very first office was little more than a twelve by twelve shack he shared with Barbara and was heated by a wood stove and oil heaters. In the summer, window fans cooled them.

From those meager beginnings, they'd grown to a modest four-office trailer complex, hiring on more and more workers every year until the last few years. Blake Industries' payroll now listed fourteen thousand employees in a town of twenty-five thousand inhabitants.

Losing contracts meant more than a slowdown in business, it meant lost jobs in a town that was still in the dawning stages of growth. The town's momentum was based on this business and he wasn't going to let that momentum falter because of some sloppy work.

Even now, he wanted to bring in his managers, go down to the factory floor, check the parts himself to see what was going on. Turning over management to another person was the most difficult decision he'd ever made.

He swiveled in his chair, his hands went to the phone, and picking it up, hovered in the air a few seconds before he dropped it back in the cradle.

He'd promised himself, and he'd promised James he'd let him handle the crisis.

After sessions with contractors to keep the last of the reports on schedule, and meetings with department heads, Johanna worked at her desk in her cabin for the remainder of the day.

It seemed every ten minutes someone was at her

door. At five-thirty another knock vibrated on the wood. Who could that be? She could usually set her clock by the time the carpenters knocked off work. They were gone. Slipping her feet into her shoes, she ran to the door and opened it to find Luke and Drucilla Jordan, the center of Nottoway society, standing on the other side.

"Hello," she said, opening the door wider and giving the couple hugs. "Come on in."

"Aren't you a sight for sore eyes?" Luke said as he escorted Mrs. Drucilla, with a hand under her elbow. She carried a brown paper bag. Luke carried a black leather briefcase in his free hand.

"You look so happy and wonderful," Johanna said to them as she closed the door.

"Go on with you," Mrs. Drucilla replied.

Everyone used the old southern vernacular when addressing her. In her mid-eighties, she didn't look a day over seventy. To say that Mrs. Drucilla stood five-three would be stretching it.

Luke stood proud and tall—at least six feet—in his black sports pants, cable-knit sweater and dark blazer. He was in his late seventies.

Mrs. Drucilla handed Johanna the paper bag. "Made some mutton last week and remembered how well you liked it."

"Thank you," Johanna took the bag and peeped inside. "I've had many fond memories of your cooking." Four tall canning jars filled the bag. "I'll return your jars to you." Johanna took one jar out of the bag and smiled. Mutton. Her favorite.

"No rush," Mrs. Drucilla said.

"Please have a seat and excuse the mess. I'm working out of the cabin as well as the hotel." Johanna led them to the sofa in front of the fireplace and looked around at swatches of fabrics for bedspreads, sofas and chairs scattered on the countertop. Other than that, the room was neat.

"Don't worry about it. You've got your work to do," Mrs. Drucilla said. "We'll make it quick." She sat on the burgundy, green and blue striped chair.

"No rush. I'm so happy to see you." Johanna sat in the burgundy overstuffed chair across from them.

Luke sat beside his wife, stretching out his long legs in front of him. "We got your message on the answering machine about the golf package. I talked to the board and they think its a great idea. It will be a big boost to our club," he said. "Even with Tiger Woods, most of the people in town don't see golf clubs as a part of their lives."

"The club package will bring more guests to the hotel. Many of the business crowd are golfers. Have you thought of prices? We're in the process of sending mailers to large corporations and travel agencies I've worked with in the past."

Setting his briefcase on his lap and opening it, Luke pulled out a manila folder and handed it to Johanna. "This is what we've worked up. The prices are negotiable. But we've looked into what other clubs are offering as part of hotel packages. We think we're in line."

Johanna opened the folder and browsed through the pages. "I can work with this." He'd also included a smart-looking brochure boasting the facilities.

"Good."

Johanna pointed to the brochure. "Can you get me enough copies of these to include in my mailer? I'll work up a price sheet from what you've given me."

Luke nodded his head. "Sounds good to me." He wrote in a small spiral notebook, then stuck it in the briefcase before closing it and dropping it back on the floor. "We've got plenty of brochures already made up. I'll have someone drop off a couple of boxes at the hotel tomorrow."

"Well, that's it for business. I've really missed you. How are you?"

"Good, good," Mrs. Drucilla said. "Luke's late with my garden but other than that I'm fine. Never going to get good peas now."

"Now, Drucilla, I told you Roger puts in a big garden every year. No need of you putting in one, too."

"I put in my own garden, Luke. Guess I'm gonna have to get Tylan to plow it up for me."

"Deg gonnit woman. I'll get your garden going tomorrow. Stubborn." He shook his head, his fondness for his wife clearly apparent in his tone.

Mrs. Drucilla tilted her chin, pursed her lips and ignored her husband. "I'm so proud of you, young lady. That hotel looks mighty good. Mighty good. Reminds me of when I was a little girl. Used to pass by and look at the fancy folks walking in, wearing their rich finery. Elonza used to make extra money then with his boat." Elonza Fortune had been Mrs. Drucilla's brother.

"He owned this boat, you see, and they'd pay him to take them fishing on the river. Some of the other boats used to ride people on the river. Catch the warm summer breeze stirring through the trees. Lord," she chuckled, "I hadn't thought of him in a long time. Forgot he even did that."

"I didn't know."

"Oh, yes. The river would be busy in the mornings. He knew the location of the best fishing holes. He was a few years older than me, you know. And sometimes on Sundays just before he docked that boat, he'd give me a ride. I'd think I was one of those fancy women, wearing an expensive hat, getting a ride down the Nottoway.'' A gleam of moisture came to her eyes and Luke put an arm around his wife's shoulder and took her hand in his big one.

"Now, now Drucilla.''

"He's been dead going on forty years now.''

"At least they're good memories,'' Johanna said quietly to comfort.

"Oh, yes. They were always good memories. He was the best big brother a sister could have. I don't know what I would have done without him after my first husband died. People look down on whiskey stills, but it sure saved us. And we weren't the only farmers it saved either.''

Luke hit his leg. "He had the best deg gone moonshine in these parts. Never could get his recipe though. Now, mine wasn't anything to turn up your nose at,'' he interjected quickly. Then he shook his gray head. "Kinda missed those days.'' A dreamy expression crossed his features.

Mrs. Drucilla tilted her head to look up at her husband. "I don't know how you could forgive me for blaming you for his death for so many years.'' Elonza Fortune had been murdered at his home and Mrs. Drucilla had believed Luke had stabbed him. Luke had been the competition.

"I love you, Drucilla,'' he said in a serious tone. "I can forgive you anything.'' He brought his hand up and tenderly caressed her cheek.

Have mercy, Johanna thought as tears glistened her eyes. To be loved like that was the epitome of life. What was life all about anyway without that special love? To have found it again in his seventies and her eighties made it all the more special.

The phone rang, severing the mood. Johanna went to answer it.

"Johanna, it's Jonathan. I'm sorry but I have to call the dinner off."

"Meeting running late?" she asked.

"Something like that." His tone wasn't his usual jovial one and Johanna frowned.

"I understand completely." She'd had a long day herself and more work to do still.

"We'll make it another time, okay?" he said.

"Sure."

He disconnected. Johanna sensed the meeting must not have been going as he wanted it to. She focused her attention on her guests.

"We have to be on our way," Luke said, standing. "It was good seeing you."

"Don't be a stranger," Mrs. Drucilla said. "Stop by and see us sometime. The new house is beside the old one."

"I will." Johanna walked the couple to their car, closing Mrs. Drucilla's door for her. As they drove off, Pam's car pulled up.

"I thought you'd be with the kids." Johanna said waiting for her.

"They're with Mom." she said and related the news about the faulty airplane part.

"Oh no." she said. "Jonathan must be worried." Wanting to comfort Jonathan immediately, Johanna frowned, thinking she'd visit him later tonight.

"James is working very late tonight. I'm going home to soak in the tub. It isn't often that I get uninterrupted time." Pam opened her car door. "The kids are spending tonight with Mom."

As Pam drove away, Johanna went into the cabin wondering if Jonathan really had a meeting or if he thought he'd be unsuitable company. He was always so thoughtful of everyone else. Who took care of him when he needed a shoulder to lean on? She'd make sure he was okay and perhaps take him dinner as well.

First she had to stop by her mom's. Earlier, Gladys had insisted Johanna come over for a few minutes.

CHAPTER 4

Wondering if she'd made the right move by visiting Jonathan, and knowing it was the only option for her, Johanna parked her car behind Jonathan's Infiniti. Opening the door, she exited her car, darkness descending on her as she shut her door.

Johanna glanced at the sky. When she'd lived in Alexandria, she was able to see only a fraction of the stars she could see here. Now they were hidden behind the descending clouds. The weatherman had predicted rain for later tonight.

The crescent moon peeking through the clouds barely illuminated the land at all. And Jonathan's white house stood out like a huge white ghost against the night.

Not another house was nearby. His place was five minutes from the hotel, but it was in a dark, deserted area at the end of the road. The three hundred acres that bordered her land belonged to him, except for the five-acre piece Smith had kept around his home.

She could hear the water from the river rushing in back of Jonathan's house. The river was one of the reasons she loved visiting this house as a child. He'd set a lawn table and chairs on the riverbank for Karina and her.

Johanna hooked her purse on her shoulder, and opened the back door to her car. Taking out the dinners her mother had packed for her when Johanna had visited an hour ago, she put the lock on the door and closed it before she remembered most of the people in Nottoway didn't lock their doors. Habits learned from living in cities wouldn't go away overnight.

She inhaled sharply, smelling the crispness of the river and pine trees. Walking carefully up the red bricked pathway, she climbed the wide steps to the huge, deep porch that spanned the front of the house. She knocked on the front door. Jonathan had never installed a doorbell to the structure that had been built in the late seventeen hundreds.

Jonathan opened the door cautiously. He was wearing old jeans and a white T-shirt. He opened the door wide, and smiled when he saw her. "Come on in."

"I was just in the neighborhood and saw a light." She passed him and walked into the huge foyer where he, Karina and she used to decorate a ten-foot Christmas tree each year. Now the area only held an antique bench and French table.

Johanna faced him after he shut the door, clutching the bag close to her. "Actually, I made a special trip to see you. I heard about your problem."

"I'm glad you came." He sniffed and glanced at her packages. "Something smells delicious," he said. "Someone looks even better. I like the rose in your hair." Johanna patted the rose she'd added as a last-minute decision.

"Mom packed leftovers." It was just like him to deviate to another topic. Always entertaining the guests, never a concern for himself, Johanna thought, wishing he'd let down his guard around her.

"I love leftovers." He closed the door. "And I haven't had dinner." He took the brown paper bags containing the platters from her.

Johanna touched his arm. "Are you okay?" She couldn't mask her concern for him.

"I'm trying to let James handle this and not worry. It's part and parcel of the business we're in."

Johanna touched his cheek. "Maybe I can take your mind off of work."

His eyes opened wider. Wrapping an arm around her waist, his eyes narrowed. He lowered his head and kissed her. "I like the sound of that already."

His half smile twisted Johanna's heart. Even as a teenager, she'd known when he was troubled just by his smile and the slant of his head. He tried to never let Karina and her know that he was distressed, but Johanna knew, and tried to console him in some ingenuous fashion. She wondered sometimes if her teenage stratagem ever worked, or if he knew.

Right now, that kiss had her heart spinning out of control while he looked calm. He led her to the formal dining room on the right, but Johanna wanted comfort not formality, and she stopped at the arched door.

"Do you mind if we eat downstairs?"

He checked himself and glanced at her. "Not at all."

Johanna led the way to the back, passing the living room on the front left. The kitchen behind the dining room was actually a bedroom he'd converted into a kitchen since, in the era the house was built, the kitchen was contained in a separate building. The den was on the back across from the kitchen.

They took the stairs, which ended in a huge great room where she and Karina had cuddled up on the couch and talked for hours as teenagers. It was a comfortable room with a huge couch and soft chairs. A small table was tucked away under a window, and an armoire held the television.

Three bedrooms, a kitchen that was built in the late eighteen hundreds with a bricked floor and two baths were on the ground-floor level. Two huge French doors allowed them to walk out onto the bricked patio in the backyard. The curtains were open, exposing the delicate windowpanes. This was the level he actually lived on.

Johanna had wondered if the decor had changed much since she'd last been there years ago. The furniture had certainly changed. Antique furniture had replaced the modern pieces. He'd often said he wanted furniture more fitting to the era rather than the modern variety.

"Bring back memories?" Jonathan asked. He'd quietly let her take her fill.

Just then, Johanna realized she'd stopped on the bottom stair, blocking the passage. She advanced farther into the room. "Yes, it does. Many fond memories."

"For me, too," he said, passing her on his way to set the platters on the table.

Johanna followed him, pulling off her jacket. "I love what you've done with this place."

"I'll give you the ten-cent tour after we eat," he offered. Let me take your jacket." He hung it on the peg nailed to the wall near the French door.

Now that Johanna was here, she was uncertain and uncomfortable when she'd never been uneasy in his home before. Before, she was Karina's friend. Now, she'd come as Jonathan's friend. The scene was totally different. And she pondered if he'd think she was too forward.

He went to the kitchen and pulled utensils out of the drawer.

"Let me help you with that." Johanna came out of her stupor and approached him.

He handed the utensils to her and pulled plates and glasses out the cabinet with a preoccupied air.

Johanna set the table and dished out the food from the containers, keeping a watchful eye on him. She was glad she'd come over.

They made small talk over dinner.

Johanna could tell he was preoccupied, but he ate all his food. He was unaccustomed to sharing his problems. Even in the past, she could only offer silent support.

Johanna didn't try to push him. The relationship was still new and she didn't quite know how to approach him.

After dinner, Johanna dug in her bag for the video she'd brought over with her. "Have you seen *How Stella Got Her Groove Back* yet?" she asked.

"No, I haven't." He leaned back against the soft sofa cushions and watched her, his hands behind his head, exposing his wide chest.

"Here we are." Walking to the armoire, she opened the double doors to reveal the television and VCR. Turning both on, she slipped the tape inside and faced him.

"It's a fun movie. I think you'll enjoy it."

"Come here." He patted the space beside him on the couch, and after lowering the recessed lights, Johanna joined him, snuggling up next to him on the overstuffed couch.

"Are you telling me I'm too staid?" he whispered next to her ear, wrapping his arms around her.

Johanna tilted her head to glance up at him. "Exactly," she said as the credits started to roll.

He lowered his head, giving her time to pull back if she wanted to. Johanna didn't want to and in seconds, his lips met hers, firm, insistent, overpowering.

There weren't many incidents in life that stole Johanna's breath. Jonathan's kiss did—a tidal wave of emotions swamped her every time she neared him.

Jonathan eased his lips from hers, knowing he should stop this before he went too far.

Johanna was Karina's friend, but he couldn't picture her as only his sister's friend any longer. He saw her as a woman—a woman he wanted in his bed. A woman he longed to be with—to *make* love with.

In a small town where secrets were few, managing an affair without adding to wagging tongues made it difficult. Thankfully, he lived at the end of a deserted road. He didn't often have company other than the triplets and Karina. But Mrs. Drucilla and Luke often stopped by to check up on him.

"The movie's starting," he whispered.

"Oh," Johanna said and faced the screen.

Jonathan kept his arm around her shoulder and settled back into the cushions.

"I'm here to comfort you, so . . . " she moved his arm and turned his back to her. Slipping off her shoes, she put one leg along the back of the chair and leaned him back against her, resting her hands on his chest. "Isn't this better?"

Amused, and touched, Jonathan thought that, stretched out between her legs and her hands raking softly through his hair was definitely better, but was it wise?

"Perfect," he said, his arms on her thighs—his

heartbeat knocking in his chest as he trailed a hand along her thigh. He didn't harbor too much hope of concentrating on the movie tonight.

In the middle of Angela Bassett's love scene, Jonathan heard a car door slam. He welcomed the diversion. Sitting up, he wiped a hand across his face and sucked in a breath. He wiped the beads of perspiration that had popped out on his forehead.

In seconds, a knock pounded on the back door.

Slowly he rose and trod to the door. Peeping through the curtains, he saw his niece shifting from foot to foot in her impatience. He opened the door to Karina and Kara.

"Hi, Uncle Jonathan," Kara said, stepping past him into the house.

She was getting prettier and taller by the day and giving her father heartaches with a sudden desire for makeup and two-hour phone conversations.

"Hi sweetheart. Where are your brothers?" Jonathan asked her.

She wore her straight hair loose and it hung past her shoulders.

"Oh, they're with Dad at some soccer meeting." She rolled her eyes. "Boring."

Jonathan ruffled her hair. Everything was boring to her these days.

"Hi, Aunt Johanna. What are you doing here?" she asked as if she had every right to.

"None of your business, young lady," Karina called after her loquacious daughter. "Hi, Jonathan. How are you, dear?" She reached up to hug him.

"I'm fine." He closed the door behind her.

"The news was the buzz of the restaurant tonight," she said, hanging her purse on one of the pegs.

"Aren't you supposed to be working now?" he asked his sister.

"Robert's taking the late shift for me. Hi, Johanna," she spoke finally, keeping an eye on her daughter.

Kara pulled a soda out the fridge. Uncle Jonathan's home was like her own.

"It's good to see you." She looked from Johanna to Jonathan. "Are we disturbing you?"

"Oh, no," Johanna answered quickly.

Jonathan reserved judgment.

Kara wandered back in and meandered over to the video. "Oh, *How Stella Got Her Groove Back*. Cool. Can I see it?" She asked, turning up the volume button on the remote control.

"May I," Jonathan corrected. Thinking of the sex scenes he'd just witnessed, he said, "No, you may not. Maybe when you graduate from college."

"You are so behind the times, Uncle Jonathan," she rolled her eyes.

"Thanks," he said, chucking her under the chin and wandering over to the television to flip it off. He shook his head. It seemed she'd grown into a new person in just one year. Where had the time gone?

"You're growing up too fast as it is," he told Kara, wondering at his sister's reaction to Johanna.

Karina only wanted his happiness, so he knew she'd be pleased. But the triplets had never seen him with a date before. No wonder Kara took Johanna's presence in stride. She probably thought Johanna was just another friend.

Sitting on the edge of the couch, looking calm and contained, with an understated sexiness, the emotions Johanna stirred in Jonathan were far from friendly.

* * *

The next morning, Johanna discovered her security guard had escorted some strange man off the property around nine the previous night. The man seemed to be loitering. Johanna wondered if it was the same man Pam had mentioned to her several days ago.

Looking at the guard's notes, she read that the man hadn't given a good reason for his presence. Most people drove by, but they didn't try to get inside the hotel and they usually visited during the day.

He'd used the excuse that he was fascinated with old buildings and how well the restoration had preserved the original architecture.

Johanna hadn't met the man, but if that was his purpose, why not visit during the day when people were around. Why skulk about at night?

Her security was warned to call the police if he was caught snooping around again.

With furniture arriving next week, she didn't want any of it leaving in the wee hours of the morning while she slept. More than one hundred beds, dressers, chairs, tables and bedside tables were due to arrive.

As soon as they'd been placed and dusted, the wall prints would be hung.

The next day, even more items would arrive. Johanna had barely any time after the exhausting days to think of anything outside of her work.

Not so for her mom who knocked on her door at seven that evening, waking Johanna who'd fallen asleep sprawled out on the couch. It took a second knock before Johanna realized what had awakened her. Getting up, she swiped a hand over her face, padded to the door and opened it.

"Hi, Mom," she said sleepily.

"You're sleeping already?" Gladys said, passing her to advance into the room. Depositing her purse on the sofa table, she glanced around the room.

"It's been a long week." Johanna took her mother's jacket and put it across a chair.

"That hotel is something else. Pamela gave me a tour while you were out today."

"I'm glad you stopped by. If you'd let me know, I would have taken you to lunch."

"I know how busy you are now with trying to get everything ready on time." Gladys made herself comfortable on the couch. "I've never seen it look so good."

"Thank you." She tried to smother a yawn.

"So, how are things going with you and Jonathan?"

So that was the purpose of her visit. "Things haven't changed between us. We're still friends just like we were when I was in high school."

"Honey, you're not a child anymore and Jonathan's a man who's been alone for far too long. Now that he's looking, you just make sure it's in your direction," she demanded staunchly. "He may as well marry you as anyone else."

"Mom," came Johanna's warning reply, "don't interfere, please."

"If I don't, you'll let someone else snatch him up. And before you know it, he'll be married to somebody else. I'm here to make sure that doesn't happen."

"If that's what he wants, there's nothing you or I can do about it."

"Don't you be stupid, girl. You're not going to find another Jonathan in your lifetime." Gladys sniffed. "Besides he doesn't know what he wants. Women have to guide men to what's best for them."

"Maybe I won't find another Jonathan," and she

agreed with her mom there. "But I can live with the decisions I make. Please, stay out of it."

Her mother tilted her chin and sniffed, ignoring everything Johanna said.

"You are coming by for Sunday dinner, aren't you? I've been wanting this for years. My whole family living near me."

"I'll be there."

"Bring Jonathan with you."

"Mom. Did you listen to anything I said?" Johanna asked, knowing her mother ignored anything she didn't want to hear.

"Every word," she assured her daughter. "I repeat, if you'd just give Jonathan more time, he'll come around. Don't let this chance pass you by. It's a once-in-a-lifetime opportunity. Now that that man's looking at you. You just make sure he looks all the way to the altar, you hear me?"

Johanna groaned. "I'm not getting married, now. We're just friends. Don't start spreading false rumors, Mom."

Gladys held up a hand. "I'm just offering him Sunday dinner, that's all." She was all innocence, and Johanna knew there wasn't an innocent bone in her mother's body.

"He doesn't need to be alone all the time. And you know his folks passed away years ago. It wouldn't hurt to invite him over to dinner." And then she tried logic. "Karina's got her own family now, and he probably feels left out going over there all the time. It wouldn't hurt to invite him one Sunday. After all, you were always underfoot in high school. You can pay him back for driving you and Karina all over the place."

Johanna threw up her hands. "All right, all right. I'll invite him."

"Good. Take his mind off his troubles." She shook her head, her tight curls flopping about. "Lord have mercy, no matter how good he is, trouble has a way of following that family."

As much of a busybody her mom was, she did have a warm heart.

Gladys stood. "I won't keep you. Get a nap, you look tuckered out. Henry is waiting for me." Johanna walked her mom to the car and once Gladys was on her way, she watched as the taillights disappeared around a curve.

Jonathan had long ago captured a tender spot in her heart that he'd never relinquished. That didn't mean he'd do anything about it. More than once, she'd wondered if he'd ever advance past the kissing and petting stage, or if she'd have to be the one to push it farther. But she didn't want to push him into anything he'd later regret.

Johanna sighed and entered the cabin. She'd get back to work.

Not five minutes after her mom left, Emmanuel stopped by wearing his police uniform.

"Hey, sis."

"And what do I owe the honor of your visit?" she asked him, suspicion narrowing her eyes. She placed her hands on her hips and waited for his reply.

"Can't a brother visit his sister?"

"I remember you from way back when, you know. What is it?" she asked him. "Come on, out with it."

"All right. I just wanted one of your hotel rooms tonight. Just one night," he said when Johanna continued to watch him with her hands on her hips.

"You can sprawl out here on the couch. It pulls out into a bed."

"It's Friday night, sis. I don't want to sleep on your couch."

"You want to stay in that big hotel all alone? Can't do. There aren't any beds."

"A cabin will do."

Johanna went to a drawer and pulled out a key. "You can use cabin number nine. Bring my key back early tomorrow," she demanded.

He lifted her up and swung her around. "Thanks, Sis." He planted a kiss on her cheek and plunked her back on her feet.

Winded, Johanna raked her hands through her tousled hair. "Did Mom order you to stay the night?"

"Mom doesn't order me around."

"Her baby? Come on," she snorted, delicately.

"Well, we heard about this man. I'll just help keep an eye on things."

Leveling a mock scowl at him, she warned, "I pay a security service to protect the property." Then she realized she was talking to his retreating back. She followed him, then waved to the young lady sitting on the passenger side waiting for Emmanuel. No wonder her couch wouldn't do.

At six the next evening, Albert Cain, the hotel's chef, who specialized in country French and American cuisine, pranced into Johanna's office waving the note she'd taped to his door early that morning. He'd been out all day on appointments with suppliers.

"Johanna," he said, strutting in, wearing his white chef's attire. "This note says you want a pig picking next Saturday night for the guests? You're joking right?" The note dangled from his fingers.

"I'm serious, Albert. Have a seat." Johanna pointed to the chair facing her desk. "That grill we had built in back of the hotel was for that purpose, remember?"

"I thought we'd barbecue chicken or grill steaks or something out there."

"No, hog roasts will be the Saturday night trademark for the hotel. Starting the weekend we open. We mentioned it in the brochure and the guests will expect it."

"Oh, gaad. I have to put the beast on that grill! Customers will have to actually see the beastly form as it cooks? Are you sure that's a sound business decision?"

"Of course and it's something we can't change now. If you can't roast a simple hog . . . " Johanna let the threat hover in the air.

"Of course I can roast a hog. I'm the best chef in the country. That's why you hired me, remember?" He sniffed, miffed at her suggestive remark.

"I knew you could, Albert." Johanna stood, signaling an end to the debate.

"But when the beastly animal spoils their appetites," Albert warned, "don't say I didn't warn you."

"The guests will wander out to see it roasting. They'll all be in awe of your skill. It'll be fun. You'll see. They don't get to experience this every day."

"I'll never eat barbecue again." He stood, executed a sharp turn and left the office, his head thrown in the air at the very idea.

Smiling at the peculiarities of chefs, Johanna picked up her purse, locked her off-white door emblazoned with a huge blue *N* and left.

Her secretary had already left. Johanna would work in her cabin tonight. But first, she drove to the One Stop Gas, Garage and Convenience Center for gas.

The yard was busy with people stopping by to fill their tanks on their way home from work. Johanna waited behind two cars before she could reach a pump. As the tank filled, she watched customers leave with Styrofoam containers of food from the hot-food concession area. She hadn't thought about dinner yet and could use a good cup of coffee to keep her alert through the next few hours of work.

After topping her tank, she parked her car in front of the store and entered the building, smiling at the tingling bell. The store was busy with people. She eased her way to the coffeepot, poured a piping-hot cup, and ordered a pork chop dinner to go before she made her way to the cashier's line.

While she stood in line, Tylan Chance walked out of his office with his son, who wore a blue jogging suit to match his dad's.

"Johanna, how does it feel being back here?" Tylan asked, hugging her.

"Like coming home." Then she looked at the pint-sized Tylan. "Your son is so precious." She stooped and was about to pick him up when she glanced at Tylan and asked, "Will he let me hold him?"

"Sure. He never misses the opportunity to be in a woman's arms. Do you sport?"

Johanna picked the child up. And the woman in back of her patted his cheek. The child leaned back to evade her touch. Johanna wanted to kiss his cheek, but didn't dare.

"Jonathan," Tylan called out, the bell announcing his arrival.

"Tylan."

"Heard about that forty-seven Dodge you bought. You going to drive it in the spring parade on Sunday?"

The library was raising funds for new books. The parade would end with a barbecue in the park. Johanna had provided two hogs for the affair.

"Sure am."

"How're Mrs. Drucilla, Luke and Clarice?" Jonathan asked him.

"They're good. Grandma's still fussing at Luke about her garden. He didn't plow a large enough space to suit her or something. I'm going to have to finish it for her this evening or none of us are going to hear the last of it."

His son was reaching for the candy on the shelves. Johanna held him just out of reach.

Jonathan laughed a rich, throaty sound.

"Ready to go, sport?" Tylan said to his son.

"No. Want candy," he said emphatically.

"Your mother will kill me if I give you candy. You won't settle down until morning."

"Uncle Jonathan. Want candy." He struggled to get down, and Johanna put him on the floor.

"Now, Tylan. How can I refuse him?"

"I'm going to let you deal with Clarice," he told his friend.

"You've got to live with her. Why don't I buy you some ice cream, sport? And you can eat it after dinner."

"Okay." He led the way to the freezer and waited for Jonathan to lift him so he could chose his own.

"He's so good with children," Johanna observed, then she glanced at Tylan. "You're certainly a good father."

"That little tyke wraps me around his finger."

"I'm all ready, Daddy," he said, immediately tearing into his Popsicle.

Tylan merely shook his head and left with his son, leaving dire threats in his wake.

"So, are you going to ride with me in the parade Sunday?" Jonathan asked, walking beside her.

"You're asking me?"

"Of course."

Johanna no longer gave wagging tongues a second

thought. "What time?" Aware that the people around them were glued to their conversation.

"Why don't we start out with church and go on from there. It's right after. Can you take the time off?"

"Even I need a day of rest."

"I'll take you to dinner after."

"I've been summoned to Mom's for dinner. You're invited, of course."

"I never turn down a home-cooked meal," he replied. Johanna wondered how long it was going to take her to get him in bed with her, and how she really felt about taking that step. From the time he entered the store, her blood pressure soared, and her body tingled.

The attraction she had for him as a teenager was just a prelude for what she felt now.

As Jonathan watched Tylan back the car out its parking space, the toddler strapped in a car seat, he thought about children of his own. He turned to Johanna and imagined her slender form rounded with child. The impact of his thoughts tightened his gut.

Children of his own had been the farthest from his mind. But a little Johanna—the thought warmed his heart. Would he make as patient a father as Henry Jones had been for Johanna?

She'd talked of her hotel aplenty while growing up. But never did she mention children.

CHAPTER 5

On Sunday morning, Johanna dressed in a green silk pantsuit in deference to the unusually cool April temperature. She wore matching leather heels and carried a green purse. A pearl necklace and earrings completed the outfit. She wouldn't have time to change after church.

Jonathan picked her up in his red and black vintage car at 10:30 for the eleven o'clock service.

"When did you get this?" Johanna asked him.

"About a year ago."

"Vintage cars are really popular now." She glanced at the dash that was so unlike today's models. "Are the seats original?" she asked, running a hand over the leather surface.

"Yes, they are. Only one man has owned this Dodge and he took excellent care of it."

It took longer than usual to reach the church. Vintage cars were nice to look at, but Johanna could really appreciate the faster modes of transportation.

The car would drive faster. Jonathan wouldn't push his "baby."

Once they arrived at church, Jonathan and she sat midway down the center aisle.

During the sermon, she felt eyes on her. But prying eyes didn't take away from the comfort she experienced sitting in the building her great-grandfather helped to build. Even by today's standards, the church was large.

Most of the people in the community attended the same church.

Luke led the congregation in the first prayer. He sat in the deacons' section while Mrs. Drucilla joined the other deacons' wives in the section across from him. She'd complained a time or two about not being able to sit with her husband, but she adhered to the old custom for Luke's sake.

Johanna's parents sat with Pamela and her family in the group of seats on the right. It was a warm day and Gladys fanned and rocked the baby, nodding her head every time the minister's message lifted her spirits.

Pastor Jacobs delivered an inspiring sermon that spoke to the young and old alike. He had a skill for delivering his message that touched the listener to the core.

After the sermon, it took a half hour of greeting people Johanna hadn't seen in years before she and Jonathan could get away to the parade.

The greetings and well wishes left a lump in Johanna's throat. She'd missed this community and these connections during her years away.

Jonathan drove through the center of town for the parade of antique cars.

The half-mile stretch of buildings included the post office, the Nottoway Bank, Pete's hardware store, the

Higabothums' Ice Cream Parlor, a yarn shop and antique stores. On the very edge, several yards away on the same side of the street were the grocery store, a cleaners and a small clothing store.

A small section in the park across the street was equipped with playground equipment. The shady trees, flowers and two picnic tables provided a respite for the lunchtime crowd. Homes bordered the opposite side of the park, most dating back to the early-to mid-nineteen hundreds.

Unseen from this point was a train track fifty feet behind the stores.

Today, the park and stores were blocked by people gathered on each side of the two-lane street that Emmanuel had closed to traffic for the parade and barbecue.

Johanna had never been prom queen but she felt special waving at the friendly crowd as Jonathan drove his car slowly down the short street behind the high school band. The parade had started nearly a mile away.

"Those are the new uniforms you bought the band. They're gorgeous," Johanna told him.

"The band's even better."

"I don't think there's anything in this town that doesn't have your stamp on it."

"I can name one," he told her, glancing at her. "The Nottoway Inn."

She laughed.

As much as Johanna enjoyed Jonathan's company, she wondered how he felt about her. She was almost afraid to think about the fact that he sought out her attention. She'd had a special feeling for Jonathan forever and was too afraid to dream that he could think of her as a woman he could love.

Sheryl had been his fiancée when Johanna was a

teenager. Sheryl had always dressed with the appropriate outfit. She always knew just the right conversational tidbit for any occasion. Johanna had envied her as a teenager. Then guilt had crowded her after Sheryl's death.

Jonathan had truly loved Sheryl. Johanna wondered if he still judged every woman against Sheryl's stellar qualities. She wondered how often he thought about what his life would have been like if Sheryl had lived.

A special connection with Jonathan was the only thing Johanna had ever wanted, but she knew he was unavailable to her. Had that changed?

He drove the car so competently. He looked so good in his suit. So commanding, yet warm; strong, yet gentle. Her insides curled just thinking about him. Johanna was afraid to get her hopes up only to discover that Jonathan couldn't love her the way she wanted him to.

One week later, water sprinkled in front of the Indian statue and freshly sprouting flowers circled it. The loading area was between the statue and the hotel, so its view was never obstructed. The front glass doors sparkled, they were so clean. Vibrant burgundy, blue and beige carpeting in the lobby gave a stately appearance. A huge Chinese vase held silver and pink Rex begonia leaves, lavender, freesia, and heather, and was prominently displayed on an antique French table.

Several groupings of conversational couches, chairs and tables were strategically placed around the lobby and in front of the oversized fireplace. The front desk, though spacious, had an Old-World welcoming appeal to it.

Coffee, punch, cookies and an assortment of hors

d'oeuvres were available for the guests in the lobby. Their experience at the Nottoway Inn would be one they would spread to their business associates and friends far and wide, Johanna hoped.

All this greeted the first guests who checked into the Nottoway Inn at eleven on Friday morning. Jonathan escorted the couple.

Johanna did the honors. She'd dreamed of this day for twenty-six years. A strong sense of contentment and a sigh raced through her that reinforced the belief that dreams did indeed come true.

"Welcome to the Nottoway Inn," she said. "You're our first guests under new management and a special gift awaits you in your suite, as well as free use of the facilities at the Nottoway Country Club for the weekend." The country club was only two miles from the hotel.

"Oh, my," the gentleman's wife exclaimed as she glanced around the lobby. "That sculpture outside. Whose work is it? The details are simply breathtaking," she exclaimed as she glanced at other art pieces in the room.

"Patrick Stone is the artist. You'll find his work showcased throughout the hotel. If you'll look in back of you near the center couch, you'll see a sculpture of Louis Armstrong who often stayed here years ago in his travels. Framed on the wall are several photographs taken of him."

"I already have one of Mr. Stone's sculptures. We purchased it two years ago when it was displayed in Jonathan's sister's restaurant. I was so taken with his work."

"He's truly a gifted artist," Johanna said.

"While we're here, I want to see every piece."

"Please do," Johanna told the woman. "And enjoy refreshments in the lobby once you're settled in."

"Thank you," she said and collected her husband who was conversing with Jonathan.

In no time, they were checked in and the bellman escorted them to their room.

Johanna left the desk to join Jonathan.

"Ummm," he groaned. "I'll have to get the golf package for them every time they have a meeting here. They're impressed with the hotel."

"And you'll be happy to purchase their package. Consider it a business expense." They started walking to her office.

"Think they'll give me a price cut on their supplies in exchange?"

"I doubt it."

Jonathan chuckled, then he said, "Thanks, Johanna. This hotel makes life so much easier for me."

"Hey, this is *my* dream, remember?"

"A dream that makes life more manageable for others." Once they reached Johanna's office, Jonathan closed the door behind him and wrapped her in his arms. He gave in to the feelings that swamped him whenever she was near.

She wrapped her hand around his neck, pulling him closer to her.

"I can't wait to see you tonight," Jonathan said when he eased his lips from hers.

"I'm getting too fond of you," she told him sliding her hands under his jacket.

"And that's exactly the way I want you." He loved the feel of her hands on him.

"Just make sure the feelings are reciprocal."

"They are," he assured her while taking little nips on her neck. Why couldn't he keep his hands off her, he wondered as he pulled her close one last time, luxuriating in her warmth pressing against him.

Jonathan finally eased his body away from hers, feeling bereft.

"I'll see you later," he promised as he opened the door and strode down the corridor.

Things were moving too quickly, he thought, but he was going to enjoy and not question what he shared with Johanna.

Johanna wasn't given long to bask in her contentment.

Plenty of work still awaited her and the refurbishment continued, though it was reduced to just the top two floors. The gardeners were hard at work coaxing the flowers along on the enormous grounds.

The implemented sales strategies had worked well. Pam and Johanna had mailed brochures and booked groups months ago based on clientele Johanna had worked with for years and who were willing to try meeting outside the DC area.

The hotel rooms booked for the weekend had been sold in packages that included hayrides through the forest, boating on the Nottoway River, golf, tennis and swimming at the country club.

Saturday night's pig roast brought most of the guests outside around the pit. Jonathan joined his guests for the buffet-styled dinner. The barbecue choices were sliced or chopped.

Albert, although he turned up his nose at the idea of a hog grilled outside, nevertheless threw himself into the task since Johanna had demanded the country tradition. Albert's attitude toward his kitchen was extremely possessive, as possessive as Johanna was about the rest of the hotel.

The rooms were booked for conventions for the next few weeks.

Johanna was well into planning for the grand opening scheduled for mid-June.

She reflected on the people who'd laughed at her as a child when she'd said she would own the hotel one day and make it the grandest hotel for a hundred miles.

They'd patted her on the head and said, "Sure you will," thinking she was as loony as her mother. She'd been true to her words.

Pleased with the success of the weekend, Johanna rose at five-thirty Monday morning to jog along the river before starting her day. But before she could get her coffee perking, she heard a car drive up next to the cabin. Peeping through the curtain, she saw Jonathan exiting the Infiniti wearing sweatpants and a T-shirt under a zippered sweatshirt. Did he look good, she thought as she followed the clean, well-built lines of his body and fanned herself.

Johanna opened the door before his first knock. "You're right on time," she said, leaning in the opening. "Let me get my key."

He approached her and kissed her—long and deep. Johanna was ready to pull him back into the cabin and forget about jogging altogether as his large hands splayed her hips and ground them against his own.

He lifted his lips an inch from hers. "Are you sure you want to go jogging?" he replied in a deep, gravelly voice that ran along her spine.

"No, but I'm sure we should."

Chuckling, he kissed her again, and Johanna could have melted into a puddle at his feet.

"Good morning," he said when he released her lips.

Darn he smelled good. "It is," Johanna said, as her imagination roamed.

"Get your key before I change my mind." He turned his back to her and Johanna ran a hand across his shoulder. His muscles tensed, and Johanna stood on tiptoe, kissing the nape of his neck before leaving him to get the key.

Taking deep breaths, she retraced her steps to join him. He'd pulled off the sweatpants and stood in shorts, the long, powerful muscles in his legs displayed.

He was warming up with stretches when she returned, and she started her own stretch routine.

"Which way?" he asked once they'd completed their warm-ups.

"Left." They started around the deck with a slow jog. He paced himself with her.

Johanna watched his long-limbed, masculine grace; his powerful thighs drew her eyes.

They were quiet for the first few minutes, as they jogged along the river. It left Johanna with plenty of time to appreciate the countryside as the songbirds serenaded them. Every morning spent with nature seemed to start the day off on the right foot—and a morning that included Jonathan topped them all.

The cool mist wrapped around them as they increased their speed.

"Has there been any progress on the filter?" Johanna asked Jonathan as she splashed through mud.

"Our engineers just got the filter. They're looking at it to see what's causing the problem."

"Oh, Jonathan, I hope it turns out well for you."

His brows creased with worry. "I'm concerned about losing contracts, or this problem preventing us from entering the Asian market," he said in cadence with their steps.

"Is it that serious already?" she asked.

"If it continues, the airline we're contracted with will drop us and use another company. It's serious," he said, tightening his jaw.

"I hope it doesn't come to that."

"So do I, Johanna, so do I."

They jogged two miles up the river and turned at an old stump that hadn't rotted away yet. Halfway back, they slowed to a walk.

Johanna knew she wasn't a pretty sight with sweat trickling between her shoulder blades. The exercise didn't take away from Jonathan's looks at all.

When they reached the cabin, Johanna cooked pancakes and turkey bacon with Jonathan's help. She didn't cook very often. But she'd cooked more since moving back to Nottoway than she had in the last ten years.

As a manager in various hotels, and since she spent such long hours there, she'd eaten most of her meals at the hotel.

When Jonathan left for home, Johanna showered and dressed for work, wondering if or when they'd cross the line to intimacy. How long were they going to kiss and try to satisfy themselves with light petting?

Then, she thought, these are the nineties, almost the end of the twentieth century. She could initiate the ascent of their relationship to another level. And she would if he didn't hurry it along. Jonathan was taking his own sweet time.

Water sluiced over Jonathan's body as he daydreamed in the shower, washing away the effects of his run. Was he moving the relationship along too slowly with Johanna? He hadn't missed the looks from other men when they were together. At the parade, more than one had looked longingly at her. He'd felt like saying, *Eat your heart out. She's all mine.* But she wasn't his quite yet. And if he moved any slower, she'd lose interest and go on to someone smoother. He wasn't smooth.

Before they took the final step, he needed to be sure. Johanna wasn't just any woman. They lived in the same small town. They'd been lifelong friends. Lifelong friends could easily become lifelong enemies if they weren't careful. Caution was the order of the day, but how he longed to get her in his bed. He wasn't waiting too much longer. Slow kisses were getting old, fast.

Maybe he should just throw caution to the wind, and let instinct take over, Jonathan thought as he stepped out the shower and grabbed a towel from the towel bar. He didn't have to think everything through in finite detail.

He pulled on underwear, trousers and a white shirt. Buttoning it, he heard a knock at the back door. He padded out the room through the great room in bare feet and opened the door to Karina.

"Hi, big brother," she greeted and passed him to hang her purse and jacket on a peg. "Haven't seen much of you lately. You've been busy?"

"Somewhat."

"I'm glad," she said, amusement dancing from her eyes as she made for the kitchen.

"I see." Jonathan buttoned his cuffs and followed her.

"I never knew you had special feelings for her." She poured two cups of coffee and offered one to him. Left unsaid was Johanna.

"I didn't until recently." He wrapped his hands around the warm cup and sipped.

Karina leaned against the countertop. "She's always worshipped the ground you walked on." Jonathan was aware that she watched him closely.

"I never knew."

"You were too busy making a living and playing Dad to me." Then the humor left her eyes. "I'm happy for you, Jonathan. She'll be good for you. She loves you."

"It's to soon for love," Jonathan said, wondering if his desire for Johanna was more than desire—if it was actually love. He weighed the word in his mind. Love was a powerful emotion. An emotion he didn't quite trust anymore.

"I know Johanna loves you. I just hope you love her, too."

"We'll see."

"Jonathan, she's the first woman you've looked at since Sheryl. I know what you had with Sheryl was special, but it's time to let her go."

"I don't love Sheryl any longer, Karina. I haven't in years."

"Well, then why hasn't there been anyone in your life? You haven't even dated in years."

"I haven't dated in one year."

"I've never met any of your friends. Where did you date? Never in Nottoway."

"No. Never in Nottoway." He shook his head and sipped on his tepid coffee. He'd always put his dates in a personal category he didn't want associated with home.

"Then where?"

"Richmond, sometimes. DC sometimes. They were never serious. I didn't love them. They didn't love me. There was no point in bringing them home."

"Jonathan, that was no way to live."

"It worked for us at that time."

"That's so sad. I thought you knew . . . "

"Karina. It's in the past."

"You feel more for Johanna, don't you?" Her troubled expression bothered him.

He nodded. "Yes, I do."

She walked over and touched his cheek with her small hand. "Jonathan, you more than anyone deserve some happiness. I hope you can love her the way she loves you. She'll always be true to you, and only you."

Jonathan sighed, the weight of what was best for Johanna weighing heavily on his shoulders. "I know that."

Karina hugged him quickly and let him go. "I have to get an order out this morning." She started to the door.

Jonathan walked her to the car and opened the door for her.

"Take care," she said, sadness for him lingering in her expression, sadness Jonathan didn't want for himself. He'd always taken care of himself. He didn't need or want her worry. He slammed her door shut and watched her back out the drive.

Johanna always loved him. He never knew that. Now that he did, what if he didn't live up to her childhood fantasies?

At ten that morning, the mail arrived and Johanna's secretary delivered it to her office. Most of it was junk, but one letter in a distinguished cream envelope was from Lewis and Hamilton, Esquire, a law firm in Philadelphia. Why would lawyers she'd never heard of be writing to her?

Picking up the letter opener, she slashed through the top, pulled the letter out and read. After the first few lines, she dropped it on the desk. Her dreams and her future quickly evaporated before her very eyes.

She scrambled through the files in her drawer, then through the filing cabinet and finally had to stop to slow the adrenaline surging through her. She needed to think. The files had to be in the cabin.

"Nancy, I'll be right back," she told her secretary as she ran out the office door, took the stairs to the bottom floor and dashed out the hotel, jogging down the pathway to her cottage.

She thought during her trek that she should have driven to work instead of taking the time to walk in. The cabin was at least a half mile from the hotel but with her harried pace, it didn't take long for her to reach it.

Her hands shaking, she slid the key into the door, opened it and ran to the office. Yanking out drawer after drawer, she finally found what she wanted. Anderson Title Company, the company she'd used to do the title search when she purchased the hotel. She located the number.

Hands still shaking, she dialed. "May I speak to Jonas Hanson, please?"

"Who's calling, please?" the receptionist asked.

"This is Johanna Jones. I'm calling about the title search you did for my hotel—the Nottoway Inn in Nottoway, Virginia."

Seconds later Jonas Hanson came on the line. "How may I help you, Ms. Jones?"

"I just received a letter from a lawyer representing a Samuel Smith that says he's part owner of the Nottoway Inn." She went on to explain the details to him.

"I need to see the letter, Ms. Jones. Can you fax it to us?"

"What is your fax number?" Johanna asked as she searched the desk for a pen and paper.

Copying the number as he rattled it off, she said, "I'll fax it to you immediately."

Johanna dashed off his name and number on the fax cover sheet and punched in the numbers. When the fax started, she tried to think of what more she could do.

"Smith," she said out loud. "He should know about this Samuel person." She flipped through the rolodex for his Florida number. Picking up the portable phone to dial it, she heard shouting and knocking at her door.

"Johanna! Open up," Pam called out. "What's going on?"

Johanna pressed the button to disconnect and carried the phone with her as she opened the door.

"What on earth is wrong?" Her expression worried, Pam jumped over the threshold. "Your secretary said you just tore out the office carrying a letter in your hand."

Johanna went into the office, grabbed the letter and handed it to Pam.

Pam glanced at Johanna and then read the letter. She staggered to a chair and sat. "Oh, no. What can you do?" she said.

Johanna slumped into the desk chair. "I've already called the title company," she stated, rubbing a hand across her forehead. "I'm going to call Smith to see what he knows about Samuel Smith and if there could be any validity to what the letter says."

"Oh, Johanna," Pamela stood and walked over to her and hugged her. "I'm so sorry. You've put your life into this hotel."

"And I'm wondering why he didn't contact me months ago or contact Smith years before. He strategically waited until I spent a fortune refurbishing this hotel before contacting me. It just isn't right."

"Go on and call. I'll wait." Pam backed up to her chair and sat on the seat's edge while Johanna punched in the Florida number.

The phone rang and rang, but no one answered. Smith didn't believe in answering machines.

Johanna disconnected. "He's out. Probably fishing. I'll try again later." Unable to sit any longer, she stood and paced the length of the office.

"You've got guests in. Do you have the money to buy him out?"

"Are you kidding? I've spent every dime I had and borrowed the rest. Smith holds a mortgage for me. The plan was for the hotel to make enough money to pay the bank and Smith off in ten years. If I lose this hotel, I'm ruined. I don't have any more money."

"He's claiming half ownership!"

"Every improvement in that building is mine," she shouted, pointing toward the hotel. "It will be a cold day in Hades before I share it with that—that opportunist."

"He could be a scam artist."

"And Anderson Title Company has some answering to do for not discovering that crucial bit of information before the sale," she said.

"Who are they?"

"They're the title company that researched ownership of the hotel."

"How could they miss information that crucial unless this Samuel person is a fake?"

"I don't know." Even now, contractors were completing the last of the renovations. Was she to stop the work at this point? She couldn't do that. She had to continue with the project to the end. And if she had to go to court, where was she going to get the money to pay for lawyers? They cost a fortune. What kind of lawyers were Lewis and Hamilton, Esquire? Were they the ambulance-chasing kind. Her case could boil down to who hired the better legal team. "I've got to make a list of things to do."

"What can I do to help you?" Pam asked.

"We have to believe we'll win this and work accordingly. In the meantime, can you recommend a lawyer in this area? I know some in DC but the case will be heard here. It's better to work with local lawyers."

"Lawyer Granger is very good. Clarice's brother, Gerald Chance, is working with him now. Give them a call. They handle Jonathan's legal work so they have to be pretty good."

"All right. I'll call them. Thanks, Pam. You've got some calls to make. I'll be all right."

"Are you sure?" her sister asked, dreading to leave her.

"Yes," Johanna nodded and reached for the phone book. She had work to do.

CHAPTER 6

Jonathan knocked on Johanna's door at five that afternoon. "I just heard," he said entering the cabin. He closed the door behind him and slid out of his suit jacket, laying it on the back of the chair.

Johanna couldn't think of anything to say to him so she remained silent.

"Have you contacted the title company?"

"As soon as I read the letter," she told him, crossing her arms in front of her.

"Smith?" He raised an eyebrow.

"I've been dialing him all day. No answer."

She paced the room, still holding the portable phone in her hand.

Jonathan caught her by the arms. "It'll work out. I'll help you."

"There's nothing you can do." She turned away to continue her pacing.

"Don't turn away from me," Jonathan said softly, coming up behind her.

"I'm not. It's just . . . " She stopped her flow of words as worry and anger mingled.

"Come here." He turned her toward him and wrapped her in his arms.

"You've got your own company to worry about," she said against his chest.

"Don't worry about that. We're doing everything that can be done."

"I have to try Smith again." She pulled away from him, punched out his number and waited while it rang six times. "Still no answer."

Jonathan took the phone out of her hand and put it on the table. "Come on. You need a break."

"I can't afford to take a break."

"You can try Smith again later. It's still early. Pam said you've talked to the title search company and a lawyer. You've done everything you can do."

"You don't understand."

"I do understand. Just take one step at a time to work through this."

"I can't think beyond this."

"Yes, you can. You aren't going to lose your business. This man is an opportunist. He's trying to cash in on your work. It won't work, Johanna. Come on. You need to get out of here." He gave her a tug. "Besides the title insurance will cover his cost."

"I forgot about the title insurance," she said, breaking away from him. She searched through her insurance papers until she found the policy. "You're right. They have to make it good."

"That's right."

"If he'll accept payment from them. Since the hotel has been renovated, it's worth a great deal more money. He may not accept payment."

"Then they go to court. It will be years before

it's settled. If he's an opportunist, he'll want a hasty settlement," Jonathan said. "Now come on."

"Where are we going?" she asked as she looked longingly at the telephone one last time. Watching it wouldn't make Smith arrive any faster.

"What would you prefer? Karina's restaurant or my place?" he asked her.

"I can't take a crowd tonight. Your place," she responded immediately.

"Get your jacket and let's go." Jonathan waited for her near the door.

They walked out into a clear, breezy evening. The brisk breeze resembled March more than April. Trees swaying in the direction of the wind reminded Johanna of how she felt, helpless to prevent whatever was happening to her.

Jonathan opened the door for her and helped her into the car before rounding the vehicle to the driver's side. The leather seats of the Infiniti were comfortable and the ride was smooth for the few minutes it took to reach his home. There was something to say about luxury cars.

Johanna inhaled sharply and went directly to the tree in his backyard. She sat in the homemade swing Jonathan had made for the triplets, feeling better than she had an hour ago.

She wondered if the children even used the swing any longer. The contraption consisted of two ropes and a wide, wooden board with groves cut out along the side for the ropes. But it was well built and comfortable and the seats had been heightened to accommodate their growth.

Jonathan watched her swing back and forth for a few minutes until he walked slowly around the back of her, grabbed the ropes and pushed her.

Many snapshots of her sister and brother swinging

with their friends came to Johanna's mind. But she was too focused on the Nottoway Inn as a child to take very much time out even for that pleasure. Did she focus her entire life on that hotel, only to have it taken away from her because of a slip-up by the title company? Johanna bit her lip to keep from crying out. Her twenty-six-year dream could be snatched away with the snap of a finger.

"You're thinking about the hotel again and not about me," Jonathan's voice intervened close to her ear. Come on." He stopped the swing. "I'm starved."

"I think about you constantly," Johanna said. Tired of tiptoeing around him, she became bold. She wanted him right now, and she didn't want to wait any longer for some nebulous time in the future.

"Do you?" He put his arms around her and held her tight, his strong arms comforting her.

"Yes, I do."

"Share your thoughts with me." Rounding the swing, he stood in front of her.

She gazed at him for a moment, the powerful male strength he exuded.

"Is it that bad?" he asked. The twisted smile he wore almost angered her.

"I don't know if you want to hear what I have to say," she said, leaning closer to him.

"Yes, I do." The smile left to be replaced by the serious tone she frequently associated with him.

"Do you still love Sheryl?" she asked. She needed an answer to that before she could move forward.

She could see that he didn't expect that particular question.

"Sheryl was an important part of my life at one time that was over a long time ago. I'm not still pining for her."

Johanna believed him but . . .

"The two of you were so . . . "

"I don't look for Sheryl in you. I care about you exactly as you are. I don't compare the two of you. And I'm not looking for a duplicate."

"I just wonder if you can love any woman after her." Johanna sighed wistfully. "She was so perfect." Johanna looked at the ground at his feet.

Her head snapped up when he pulled her to her feet. Putting his strong hands on her cheeks, he tilted her face until she gazed directly into his eyes. The icy determination in his gaze puzzled her.

"Nobody's perfect Johanna. Not me, not you and neither was Sheryl. We all have our faults. Loving someone is the joint acceptance of both of your faults." He pulled her closer to him, moved his hand behind her head, and pressed his lips against hers.

With the warmth seeping from his body to hers, she just realized how much the temperature had dropped and how well he heated her blood.

All those times she'd seen him with Sheryl, wishing she could have his undivided attention, melted away with his hard strength pressing against her. Although he touched her and kissed her, he'd never asked to complete their union. Johanna wanted all of him. She wanted completion and she wanted it tonight.

"Jonathan," she whispered against his ear when their lips parted. His gray gaze melted into hers just before his tongue touched her ear.

"What?" he whispered, his hot breath heating her blood by twenty degrees.

"I . . . nothing," she said, pulling his shirt out of his pants and sliding her hands underneath it. She felt the hard strength of his rippling muscles. She'd let her fingers and her body do the talking tonight.

She rocked against him, eliciting a primal moan from deep within him.

Her head swam, her heartbeat slammed against her chest. Johanna's center fluttered like a million butterflies were attacking her midsection at once.

His hands lifted her shirt, cupped one of her breasts, stroking it with his thumb. He bent closer and his hot breath caressed her skin a second before his lips closed around a nipple straining against the bra.

Johanna couldn't stop the moan that escaped her lips—didn't want to. Her boneless knees would cease to support her any second now. Only the pressure from his hands splayed around her waist kept her upright on legs, trembling with need.

She circled her hand around his neck, then stroked the rippling shoulder muscles. The texture of his skin, masculine and hard, drove her desire higher and higher.

At that very moment, she needed him like life-sustaining oxygen.

"Jonathan," she whispered.

He lifted her breasts from the bra, stroking them back and forth with his mouth and fingers, his hot breath a perfect contrast to the lowering temperature.

"Jonathan," she whispered again, wanting more—needing more of him.

He lifted his head, and his eyes, dazed and glassy met hers, every fiber of his need pouring from them. Then his mouth was on hers, insistent, hot and hard. He thrust his tongue into her mouth and mated with her own.

Savoring his taste, she sucked on his tongue, eliciting a low groan from deep within him.

His arms pulled her tighter against him, her breasts buried against his chest.

She cried out at the friction of skin and hair rubbed against her sensitized nipples. Her arms held him tightly and his hands went to her buttocks, grinding her softness against the hardness of his manhood.

She wanted all of him.

It was a moment before she realized his mouth had parted from hers.

"We've got to stop," he rasped, sounding so unlike the Jonathan she'd known forever.

"Why?" her confused brain couldn't interpret as he loosened his hold on her, but still held her loosely in his arms. He didn't let her go.

As seconds ticked by, the cool air seeped into her consciousness. When he finally released her completely, Johanna took a step back.

Jonathan inhaled sharply. "I'll . . . ah." He took a moment to wipe a hand across his face and blew out a long breath. "I'll cook dinner."

"Dinner?" Johanna repeated stupidly. Why was he talking about dinner when she wanted to charge into his house and to his bed and complete what they'd started. She needed to feel his body pressed against hers—his body in hers. She gulped a fresh lungful of air.

The cold seeped more and more into her. Realizing she stood exposed to him, she struggled to fix her clothing. Embarrassment mixed with need when she realized how much she wanted him and how cool he stood looking away from her.

"The heck with dinner, and with you," she shouted. "I'm going home."

"Don't." One long arm extended to stop her before she could take one step. "We aren't ready for the next step, Johanna. Think about it."

"You mean *you* aren't ready. Do you really think I'd let you touch me like that if I weren't ready?"

When he remained silent, she shoved a finger at his chest. "Tell you what. You let me know when you get Sheryl out of your system. And don't think I'm going to wait another decade, either." Johanna detached herself, walked around him and moved steadily toward the driveway.

"You haven't had dinner," was his lame comeback.

"I've got a chef capable of preparing me any meal I want," she snapped.

"Let me explain." When she stopped short, Jonathan almost ran into her.

"Explain what? That you wish you were with Sheryl every time you're near me?"

"Of course not! I'm with you, aren't I?" He took her hand in his. She snatched it back and placed it on her hip.

Glancing at the ground and struggling for control, she pierced him with her gaze.

"You may not want to, but you are."

"This situation is blowing all out of proportion," he said, "just because I want to wait."

"We agree on that, at least." Johanna resumed her trek to the car, then realized she hadn't driven. She bypassed it and started walking to the road.

"Good-bye, Jonathan," she said.

He sighed heavily and grabbed her arm. Taking her hand, he gave her the keys to his Infiniti and closed her fist. "I'll call you," he said.

Johanna started to throw his keys back at him, then she thought about the long walk home. She opened the door and entered the car, sitting on a seat that cushioned her behind like a glove. Inserting the key in the ignition, she started the motor and roared out the drive.

With a start, she realized that not once had she thought of stocks, her portfolio or the Dow Jones averages during their brief lovemaking as the soft Nottoway winds blew over their heated bodies.

* * *

Watching her leave, Jonathan wanted to grab her and hold on. How could he explain to her that he couldn't take advantage of her while she was so troubled? She'd only hate him later, wondering what kind of man would make love to a woman for the first time when loving was the farthest from her mind?

Wanting Sheryl? Damnation, he was so hot for Johanna, it took every last ounce of determination to keep from dragging her into the house, stripping every stitch from her body and exploring to his body's content and then, he'd . . . He swore. He was as hard as a brick!

If—when—he and Johanna reached that point, he wanted their passion to emerge from a driving desire that bordered on desperation. He wouldn't abide intimacy with Johanna simply as a means to forget the present for a short time. There would be no more faking love. He wanted every emotion to be real and for him alone. Not something she settled for because of the moment, or her mother or just to have a warm body pressing close.

Jonathan groaned, turned, and walked toward his beloved Nottoway River. Even that wouldn't calm the desire raging through his body.

Driving back to the hotel with the window open had the effect of cooling Johanna's temper several degrees. But food was the farthest from her mind. Food couldn't compensate for a passionate sexual release in Jonathan's arms.

Parking in front of her cabin, it took only a few seconds for her to go in and she immediately dialed

Smith's Florida number. He was finally home and she explained the situation.

"I was the only offspring from my family," he said. "My uncle had no children. He never married," he told her.

"Well, the letter stated that Samuel Smith is your uncle's grandchild."

"I've saved every scrap of paper from way back when. I'll look into it. Don't you worry, Johanna. Nobody's going to take that hotel from you. It's yours. You've earned it," he assured her.

"Thanks, Smith."

Lowering the phone to the cradle, Johanna realized Smith's words did little to comfort her. If this supposed relative started to make trouble for her, none of the good intentions and kind words would work in a court of law.

Then she wondered what Smith had stashed away in his row upon row of boxes to disprove his cousin's claim, if Samuel was indeed his cousin.

The phone rang. Johanna lifted the receiver, hoping it was Smith with some favorable news.

"Hello?" she responded.

"Are you all right?" Jonathan's concerned voice still had the effect of accelerating her heartbeat, even after their recent encounter.

"I'm fine," she said, annoyed with her body's reaction to his voice.

"Johanna. You're special to me. I'm taking it slowly because I don't want to make any mistakes with you. I don't want there to ever be regrets with us. Which would happen if I rushed you into intimacy."

"I could never regret what we have. You can be cautious to a fault, you know. When you're dealing with people you can't dot all the I's and cross all the

T's. You've just got to trust at some point. And if I get hurt in the meantime, I won't like it, but I'll get over it."

"I could never hurt you."

"If you don't let your obsession with Sheryl go, I will be hurt. It's past time."

"This obsession is all in your mind. Trust me enough not to subject you to a relationship when I'm pining after another woman."

Johanna refrained from commenting. She'd reserve judgment on that point.

"One day, you'll believe me," he said.

Johanna was silent. She knew he and Sheryl had that special connection few couples achieved. A connection she longed to experience with him.

"Friday night is the grand opening for the new movie theater in town. Will you go with me?"

"Yes, I'll go," she responded. Why couldn't she say no to him? Where was her backbone?

The theater was swamped with every politician and mover and shaker in Nottoway. An increase in size from seating for one theater to three was an event worthy enough to bring out a reporter from the *Nottoway News*.

The line of local residents wrapped around the building as people crowded to see the first showing.

Johanna and Jonathan were in line behind the mayor and his wife, Tina. They'd married only a year ago and Tina was in her element as a politician's wife.

"Oh, dear. It's so good to see you, Jonathan and Johanna," Tina said. "I've heard the two of you have become quite an item." She patted Jonathan on the arm. "It was so good of you to donate the new tables for the nursery school. They've needed the furniture desperately," she said. She always gave proper attention to her new husband's constituents. "And it's so good to see you dating again. I thought you'd never get over Sheryl." She shook her head in regret. "I did enjoy working with her on charitable activities just shortly before her departure," Tina said as though Sheryl had taken off to a new town instead of the hereafter. "She was so good at organizing. Something I'm absolutely terrible at. She would have made the perfect businessman's wife. That year she worked on the save the rescue squad drive, we raised virtually a fortune. She had everything planned to the very last detail and it went so smoothly. It hasn't run that smoothly since. Dear Jonathan," she said still holding his hand, "I know how you must have missed her terribly."

Then she smiled. "But little Johanna was always a dear, unassuming child. You've done such a marvelous job on that hotel. You've made it into something the town can truly be proud of instead of the ghastly treatment it received all these years with Smith."

"Thank you." The joy of seeing the movie had evaporated, leaving a pall on the evening. Sheryl again. It has taken fourteen years for Jonathan to get over her. No wonder he still pined for her with people like Tina around to remind him of her constantly. Now, they reminded Johanna as well.

The phone was ringing as Jonathan entered his house. He dropped his bag of groceries on the couch and hurried to answer it.

"Hello?"

"Jonathan," James said. "The engineers have examined the filters. The bad ones weren't made by

Blake Industries. It wasn't what we shipped to the distributor."

"How did the mix-up occur?"

"They're checking their records, and will get back to us soon."

CHAPTER 7

By seven Monday morning, Johanna had narrowed her choices for the invitations for the grand opening down to three. Blue, green and mauve invitations were propped on the desk in front of her. She'd promised Pam she'd make her decision by lunchtime.

Now she vowed she wouldn't move from her seat until she'd chosen. As she thought about the pluses of each one, the ringing phone intruded on her thoughts.

"Johanna?" her mom's worried, breathless voice carried over the wire.

"Good morning, Mom." Johanna forced more enthusiasm into her voice than she felt. Just because she was down in the dumps didn't mean she had to spread it.

"I just heard. Lord, how could Smith get you tangled up in this mess and let you spend all that money? He had to know he had kinfolk who shared in that property. He just wanted to get away to do his fishing, leaving you to worry about dealing with his folks.''

At a sharp intake of breath, Johanna cut in.

"Mom, it wasn't like that at all.'' Johanna had tried to keep the info about the hotel quiet, at least for a while. "Smith didn't know this man existed. I . . . ''

"Don't count on it," her mom replied. "He knew that his family was broke—have been since the crash in the thirties. They didn't have the money to refurbish the hotel and he knew he'd be stuck here with it forever. Now that he's loaded it off on you and stuck you with this problem, he has the money to buy a house in Florida and live the good life, leaving you with nothing but worries.''

"Mom, think about what you're saying. It was Smith who bought my first shares of Coca Cola in the sixties. Every year he'd buy at least one hundred shares of some stock, sometimes more for me. Why would he do that if he wanted to cheat me?" Johanna reasoned as she put her elbow on the desk and leaned her head against her hand. "He taught me all I know about stocks so that when I started working, I knew how to choose my own. Why would he do that to trick me?''

"Johanna, even when you were seven, you ran that front desk, checking the customers into the rooms like a pro and made sure Smith made enough repairs and kept the place halfway decent enough for people to stay in," her mother admonished. "The hotel has been run-down forever. Who was going to buy it from him if not you?''

"I loved working here. He knew that and so did you," she said. Leaning back into her padded seat, Johanna glanced at the clock. She needed to make her decision and get to the hotel quickly.

"Humph. The few little improvements that got

made, you made them, telling him when you were twelve that he needed to fix this or that. You earned those measly shares of stock he gave you. You know you worked for that money. And over my objections, too, if you'll remember. But when I said something to your daddy about it, he'd say, 'it's harmless enough. Go on and let the girl tinker around the place.'"

"Mom, Smith has always hated the hotel business. He didn't love it the way I do. He held on to it for me. He could have sold it years ago if he'd wanted to." Johanna sighed. She wasn't in the mood to deal with this today. "But Smith wanted to pass it down to someone in the family that had a real attachment to it, not to someone who could care less about it the way he did. You know that."

"Distant relative, may I remind you. This cousin of his is a close relative and in the courts, his kinship is the one that will count. I still say you earned whatever you got. And look at all the money you had to put into it to get it fixed up. And now you could lose the whole thing."

"That's not true. I have title insurance. The insurance company will have to investigate and pay, but only if this man is actually entitled. That has to be proven."

"But it's still one more headache for you. And don't you tell me you aren't worrying because I know you. You worry about everything."

Just as her mother worried over every ordeal, Johanna thought.

"It's my hotel. Of course I worry. But it's part and parcel for being in business. Smith can't do anything about that."

Silence stretched a few seconds and Johanna glanced at her invitations again.

"What does Jonathan say about it?"

"He tells me not to worry. And that's exactly what I'm going to do. I don't want you to worry either. And Mom, please don't spread tales about Smith because he wasn't responsible for this man's actions."

Her mother snorted. "You're entitled to your opinion and I'm entitled to mine."

"As long as you don't repeat them. Please don't go spreading false tales."

"I'm not a gossip, Johanna. What do you take me for? I always have your best interest in mind. You know that," she said in an aggrieved tone.

"I know, Mom."

"Well, I guess I'll go get the ingredients for the birthday cake I'm making for Nicole. She'll be sixteen Wednesday. Did you know that?"

"Yes I do." Johanna realized she hadn't purchased a gift yet.

"I'm going to surprise her and take it to school. They can sing 'Happy Birthday' to her in class."

Johanna sucked in a cautious breath. "Mom, hold the cake for after school. They don't sing 'Happy Birthday' to students in high school. Just in elementary school."

Johanna heard her mother *tsk*ing over the phone.

"She wasn't here in elementary school, Johanna. So I couldn't do it then, now could I? But I can make up for it now," her mom assured her.

"Mom, you'll embarrass her. You know how sensitive teenagers are. I'll come over for dinner. So will Emmanuel. You can make a big family to-do with it. But, don't take the cake to school."

Gladys' sigh resounded clearly in Johanna's ear.

"They're all growing up too fast. Johanna, why don't you go on and marry Jonathan. I always wanted to take cakes to school for my grandchildren."

"I don't have time for babies right now." She

jumped at the opportunity to pay her brother back for all their childhood misgivings. "Maybe Emmanuel will give you grandchildren one day."

"Oh, he's still young and sowing his oats." Her wistful sigh came clearly over the wire again. "Jonathan needs a wife. All that money. We may as well have it in this family. And he's a good man. He'll never mistreat you."

"I don't need to marry Jonathan for money. I have my own. Besides, I've always taken care of myself."

"Doesn't hurt to have a man's strong shoulders to rest your head on now and again. Owning that hotel can't give you that kind of peace."

"Let me worry about marriage. It's just not on the agenda right now."

"Agenda? You had better get off that business kick and worry about getting that man for a husband. Make some time for him. Fix him dinner. You know how to win him over." She paused. "Then, too, you weren't ever much for courting. Never fear, I can give you some hints."

"That's okay, Mom. I know what to do. I'm thirty-three, you know."

"Are you sure that you do? I married your dad straight out of high school. Heavens, child, by thirty-three I had three children."

"I'm sure I know what to do." Three children running around Johanna would drive her crazy. She could only tolerate one of Pamela's at a time.

"If you need any help, let me know. In the meantime, invite Jonathan over on Wednesday for Nicole's birthday celebration. He'll come if you ask him."

"Check with Pam first, Mom. Make sure Nicole doesn't have a date that night."

"Lord, She's too young to date, Johanna. Where has the time gone?" she said almost to herself. "Anyway, this is family. A date can wait. Day after tomorrow, I'll fix a dinner you can take to Jonathan. It will make him feel good.''

"Mom, the hotel kitchen is open. I can get the chef to fix a dinner if I wanted one.''

"It's not the same as home cooking.''

"Let me worry about Jonathan. Sometimes being too aggressive can turn a man away.''

"If I let you worry, he'll be on to the next woman while your head is stuck in those hotel accounting books, young lady. I'm only trying to help.''

Johanna glanced at her invitations and her watch. Time passed quickly. " 'Bye, Mom,'' she said, trying to urge her mother off the phone. "I've got to get to work.''

" 'Bye, darling. I'll see you Wednesday.''

"Do you need me to bring anything?'' Johanna asked as an afterthought. Albert would come up with something special to whip up for her.

"I've got it all taken care of.''

"All right, then.'' Johanna disconnected.

She couldn't go another minute without her coffee. She made a quick dash into the kitchen to pour it, then returned to her desk to make her decision.

The blue card bespoke an understated elegance, the mauve was flashy but warm, and the green was refreshing. Johanna contemplated which one best suited the hotel and she realized all three would fit the decor. The ambiance was warm and inviting while still preserving the understated elegance of a world-class resort.

The marvelous grounds and the Nottoway River presented a refreshing experience for the world-weary vacationers who sought to escape their everyday lives. But above all, with the elegant structure of meeting rooms and presidential suites, Johanna realized the blue invitation would suit the hotel's charm best of all.

"Blue it is," she decided, scooting back the chair and rising from the desk.

Johanna finished drinking her cup of coffee before she donned the jacket to her navy suit, glancing at her watch one last time.

She had a packed schedule this morning—a planning session with all the managers to finalize the plans for the grand opening scheduled for June, would take most of the day.

"I'm going to hassle you for the rest of your life if you were the one who told Mom about Smith's cousin," Johanna said to Pam an hour later.

They met in the meeting room in one of the two executive suites in the hotel. This suite consisted of two bedrooms—one with a king-size bed and Jacuzzi, the other with two double beds, a formal dining room, a meeting room, a bar in the den and full-service kitchen with walk-in refrigerator and freezer, and three baths.

The other suite wasn't quite as elaborate.

The other meeting rooms were being used by clients today. The hotel had run with a ninety to one hundred percent occupancy since the doors opened, an occupancy rate any hotel owner would be proud to boast.

Pam held up both hands and shook her head. "It wasn't me. Are you kidding?"

"Somebody did. She had me on the phone half an hour this morning." Johanna dropped her pad with the notes and papers the secretary had typed for her on the table. Rising from her chair, she went to the sideboard and poured coffee.

"And she carried on as usual." Pam knew their mom's tendencies.

Johanna nodded, and returning to her seat, she sipped her coffee. "What does Nicole want for her birthday? I have to shop this evening."

"Something small will do," Pam said. "I've gotten her gifts already."

"She'll never forgive me if I didn't get her something special. It's hard to know what they like at this age. Teenagers today are so picky."

"They grow up so fast. She's a junior next year. Two more years and she'll be out of the house. It seems like yesterday when she was just a baby." A suspicious shininess appeared in Pam's eyes.

"Growing pains," Johanna bemoaned. Her mother still had trouble severing the ties.

"I don't know if I'm ready for her to leave." Pam raked a hand through her shoulder-length hair, so much like her daughter's.

"You've raised her to be the perfect young lady. She'll be fine. Your relationship will change, but you'll always be close."

"I hope I won't be as smothering as Mom," Pam lamented, shaking her head.

"You won't be." Johanna shook her head at the thought. "Mom's encouraging me to marry Jonathan and produce a few grandchildren to add to yours."

Pam smiled. "You could do worse."

Johanna sighed and moved to the chair at the head of the table, and frowned. "I think Jonathan's still in love with Sheryl."

Pam narrowed her eyes, shaking her head. "No, he isn't. He's not the kind of man who would end his life with Sheryl's death."

"It's taken him so long to get over her. I still don't think he is."

"He also isn't the kind of man who plays around. If he isn't serious about a relationship, he's not going to waste his time or yours," Pam assured her. "How do you feel about him? I know you had that high school crush on him."

"Ummm, don't ask," Johanna groaned. "I didn't think anyone knew about that," she sighed. "But now, I think my feelings are more than they should be. I'm cautious, though. I want to know that he's completely over Sheryl before I open myself to him," if she wasn't already too late.

"Sometimes, sister of mine, you tend to be way too cautious. Throw that caution to the wind and go by instinct for a change. Sometimes you just have to take a chance."

Johanna remembered the last time she threw caution to the wind and wound up frostbitten in the process. She worked in sales at the time, dating another colleague in the same position in the office— a definite no-no in the business world. When another hotel in the chain offered a promotion, he told the general manager of the hotel that Johanna wasn't interested. Management had offered the position to her anyway, which she accepted.

Gary had used the excuse that if they married, she would follow him, that she couldn't expect him to follow her. Johanna had no intentions of getting married and would never even consider marrying a man so deceitful. If he couldn't be honest with her, she wanted no relationship with him. The promotion had secured her a director of sales position in a California hotel. One where she had gained enormous experience in and had been successful at. From there, she'd gone on to become food and beverage manager and later, general manager of the hotel.

Albert's distinct voice brought Johanna's thoughts

back to the present. He strutted in, wearing his usual white from head to toe. Johanna stood and clapped. "At checkout, everyone raved about the pig roast, Albert. 'An elegant country affair,' was quoted in the style section of the Sunday *Nottoway News*."

Albert took a bow. "Never let it be said that I can't rise to the occasion," he said, bowed again, and continued to his seat.

"Your pig roast will be the talk of every weekend guest at the hotel for years to come all across the country. You're a legend already," Pam assured him.

"If I must do the beastly labor, then I will certainly make sure it is the absolute best presentation possible."

"Why, thank you, Albert," Johanna said.

Johanna's secretary strolled in with pad, pen and tape recorder followed by the other managers.

"Now that everyone's here, let's get started," Johanna said, looking forward to getting the grand opening plans finalized at last.

This week the tuxedos and formal attire had to be ordered. This was a last brainstorming session on political figures, media, corporations, travel agencies and local citizens who would be mailed invitations. Everything had to be decided.

Albert needed the count on food to put together contracts needed to be negotiated with other restaurants and caterers in the area. As well as bands for both outside and the indoor lounge areas.

Nottoway would see the inn at its finest in June.

CHAPTER 8

When the phone rang, Jonathan's secretary was out of the office. Since he was expecting a call from James, he picked up his own line. When silence greeted him after he spoke, he started muttering an oath and barely checked himself from returning the receiver to the hook when he heard a cautious, "Jonathan?"

He immediately recognized Mrs. Jones' voice.

"Good morning, Mrs. Jones." He leaned back in his chair, impatiently gripping the phone.

"I know you're busy, so I'll make it quick," she told him. "I'm so worried about Johanna and this business with Smith's cousin."

"There's nothing to worry about, Mrs. Jones," he assured her. "Did Johanna explain to you that she'd purchased title insurance for the hotel and that company will handle the costs, if any, and the fee for the lawyer?"

"I don't know much about this business stuff. And I just wanted to make sure everything's under control with Johanna. You know how to talk to and deal with these people. You've had to handle just about everything since you've been in business."

"Take my word for it, Johanna's on top of the situation," he reassured her.

"You've looked into the matter, you say?" She paused while waiting for his answer. She usually talked so much she barely gave anyone else a chance to talk.

"Johanna is quite capable of handling her own business," Jonathan told her.

"Still, I'll feel better if you look into it. Women don't always get the treatment men do, you know. And your being a successful businessman has some clout in this town," she continued.

"Don't worry, Mrs. Jones. Like I said, Johanna has everything under control. Have you talked about this to her?" Jonathan was sure she had.

"I talked to her. She seemed worried. Maybe you should talk to her, too."

"We've already discussed it and all is well."

"Well, if you say so," she paused for several seconds. "Pamela's oldest daughter has a birthday Wednesday. I'm throwing a little party for her. I was wondering if you could come by? Just as a family friend."

"Thank you for inviting me. I'll try to make it," Jonathan glanced at his watch. What was keeping James?

"Good. I feel like you're one of the family already." Jonathan could almost hear her smile.

"Thank you, Mrs. Jones." He drummed his fingertips on the desktop.

"You're welcome, dear."

Jonathan disconnected thinking that the pressure was on for marrying Johanna. He stirred the idea around. Marriage to Johanna. What would it be like coming home to her each evening? She wouldn't be

heart & soul

1 year (6 issues) $16.97 plus receive a FREE HEART & SOUL
Healthy Living Journal with your paid subscription.

YES! I want to invest in myself and subscribe to HEART & SOUL, the health, fitness and beauty magazine for savvy African-American women. I'll get a year's worth of helpful information that will inspire me to discover new ways of improving my body...my spirit...and my mind. Plus, I'll get a **FREE HEART & SOUL** *Healthy Living Journal* to keep a daily record of my wonderful progress.

Name _____ (First) _____ (Last)

Address _____ Apt #

City _____ State _____ Zip _____   MABL6

☐ Payment enclosed   ☐ Bill me
Rush my HEART & SOUL
Healthy Living Journal

Please allow 6-8 weeks for receipt of first issue. In Canada: CDN $19.97 (includes GST). Payment in U.S. currency must accompany all Canadian orders. Basic subscription rate: 6 issues $16.97.

BUSINESS REPLY MAIL

FIRST-CLASS MAIL   PERMIT NO. 272   RED OAK, IA

POSTAGE WILL BE PAID BY ADDRESSEE

heart&soul

P O BOX 7423
RED OAK IA 51591-2423

An important message from the ARABESQUE Editor

Dear Arabesque Reader,

Because you've chosen to read one of our Arabesque romance novels, we'd like to say "thank you"! And, as a special way to thank you, we've selected two more of the books you love so well to send you absolutely FREE!

Please enjoy them with our compliments, and thank you for continuing to enjoy Arabesque...the soul of romance.

Karen R. Thomas

Karen Thomas
Senior Editor,
Arabesque Romance Novels

3 QUICK STEPS
TO RECEIVE YOUR FREE "THANK YOU" GIFT
FROM THE EDITOR

Send back this card and you'll receive 2 Arabesque novels—
absolutely free! These books have a combined cover price of
$10.00 or more, but they are yours to keep absolutely free.

There's no catch. You're under no obligation to buy anything.
We charge nothing for the books—ZERO—for your 2 free
books (except $1.50 for shipping and handling). And you
don't have to make any minimum number of purchases—
not even one!

We hope that after receiving your free books you'll want to
remain an Arabesque subscriber. But the choice is yours to
continue or cancel, anytime at all! So why not take us up on
our invitation to receive your free gift, with no risk of any
kind. You'll be glad you did!

Call us
TOLL-FREE
at 1-888-345-BOOK

THE EDITOR'S FREE "THANK YOU"GIFT INCLUDES:
2 books delivered ABSOLUTELY FREE (plus $1.50 for shipping and handling

A FREE newsletter, Arabesque Romance News, filled with author
interviews, book previews, special offers, BET "Buy The Book"
information, and more!

No risks or obligations. You're free to cancel whenever you wish . . .
with no questions asked

FREE BOOK CERTIFICATE

Yes! Please send me 2 free Arabesque books. I understand I am under no
obligation to purchase any books, as explained on the back of this card.

Name _____

Address _____ Apt. _____

City _____ State _____ Zip _____

Telephone ( ) _____

Signature _____
Offer limited to one per household and not valid to current subscribers. All orders subject
to approval. Terms, offer, & price subject to change.

AB0999

Thank you!

Accepting the two introductory free books places you under no obligation to buy anything. You may keep the books and return the shipping statement marked "cancel". If you do not cancel, about a month later we will send 4 additional Arabesque novels, and bill you a preferred subscriber's price of just $4.00 per title (plus a small shipping and handling fee). That's $16.00 for all 4 books for a savings of 25% off the publisher's price. You may cancel at any time, but if you choose to continue, every month we'll send you 4 more books, which you may either purchas at the preferred discount price. . .or return to us and cancel your subscription.

THE ARABESQUE ROMANCE CLUB
c/o ZEBRA HOME SUBSCRIPTION SERVICE, INC.
120 BRIGHTON ROAD
P.O. BOX 5214
CLIFTON, NEW JERSEY 07015-5214

AFFIX
STAMP
HERE

stifling, that's for sure. He'd have his freedom to work without a lot of explaining if a business meeting ran late or a project required enormous overtime. The idea wasn't unpalatable at all. But this time around he wanted to take his time in making such an enormous decision. He wanted to really get to know the woman first.

Although he wasn't in love with Sheryl any longer, thoughts of marriage brought back dismal images of his engagement to her. Images he wished he could forget and, yet couldn't. But there were some good memories that didn't quite overshadow the displeasing ones.

Johanna had come home the weekend of his wedding and had spent lots of time with Karina. He remembered feeling more lighthearted than he'd felt since she'd left for college. The first week she and Karina were away, the house seemed so lonely, he could barely stand it. He wondered if he'd finally asked Sheryl to marry him because he was lonely and alone in his house that was tucked away in the forest.

He remembered one disturbing conversation with Sheryl that should have given him more insight into her character. But his mind had been more on his company and the future than on what was wrong with his engagement.

She'd wanted new furniture for the house.

"Sheryl," he'd said patiently, "I can't afford an eight thousand dollar living room suit and another fourteen thousand for a dining room set right now. Maybe in a year or so, but not now."

She ran a hand over his chest, tangling her fingers in his hairs. "Why not, Jonathan? You own your own business. You have more than two thousand employees. Surely you can afford a little money for new furniture and remodeling if we must live in this dreadfully old house."

He liked the house just fine. He thought it had character and the structure was sound—more sound than any new house he could buy today.

He embraced her and lifted her face toward him. "Honey, this is a big expansion, the largest one yet. It will allow me to double the business. I'll be able to hire another two thousand people," he told her. "Nottoway needs an economic base with stable jobs for the town to flourish. We'll be on the cutting edge of that growth. You understand, don't you, sweetheart? As my wife you'll be part of this expansion. I'll like having my wife close to me at the office."

She smiled and when Jonathan gazed at her beautiful pleasant expression, he realized it was the same front she used for any number of business associates he'd introduced her to. But he was her fiancé. Surely there should be love in her eyes.

"Of course I understand, but honey I'm not going to work after we marry. I'll have to deal with the social aspect of your business," she said.

"I hadn't thought of that, but you're right. I hate dealing with politicians and such."

So pleased that she was finally agreeable to waiting, he said, "Without growth, our young people will have no recourse but to move away to earn a decent living."

"But surely a little money will be left. You entertain politicians and businessmen. How can I entertain in this old house with rundown furniture?"

He wondered if she'd heard a word he'd said. He paid a fortune for the wedding as it was. And the furniture was just fine. Nice and sturdy.

"Perhaps if we'd had a smaller wedding, we'd have enough left over." Jonathan sighed. "Maybe we can have this reupholstered or we can buy something a little cheaper.'' Why had he never seen this side of her before? Was he so focused on work, he hardly knew the woman he was about to marry?

She'd touched his cheek and kissed his lips. "Honey, you're an up-and-coming businessman. We had to invite the business community. We had to invite all the right people. Our wedding is a business move as well as a personal occasion for us.''

He realized that Sheryl was the perfect social wife. And she loved him to boot. She'd make sure he invited the right people, served on the charitable boards. She would cover the bases that he didn't have the time to cover.

His dream was to make Nottoway the best self-supporting town in Virginia. One that any family would be proud to live in. Safe, secure and culturally enriched.

A week later, he and Sheryl had just had another argument about purchasing new furniture for the house when Johanna walked in. Even as a teenager, she could care less about the latest fad, furniture or house. She was focused on her beloved Nottoway Inn. She understood his dreams because she had dreams of her own and they often conversed about them.

She'd talked to him for two hours one afternoon while she waited for Karina to return from the seamstress—he spinning his dreams of expansion at his company, she spinning hers of owning her own hotel and how she'd refurbish it, her sales tactics. He felt a certain kinship with her.

Then he began to question his relationship with Sheryl. Was what they shared really love? Did she love him, the man, or the successful business tycoon? Did she have dreams beyond their marriage and social standing?

It was the eve of their wedding when he'd discovered that it had been the business tycoon and the success it would bring her that she loved, not him at all.

Jonathan refused to go into that kind of marriage. He'd rather go it alone.

His parents had married for love and whatever problems they'd weathered were solvable because they first loved each other.

At twenty-eight, Jonathan wasn't a fresh kid who believed that love solved everything. But if the marriage had a strong base and value system with love and support to enhance it, then everyday problems were solvable if the parties involved were willing to allow the time and had the determination to work it through.

The phone rang again bringing him to the present. When it stopped immediately, he realized Barbara was back.

"James on line two," she said.

Jonathan pressed the button.

"James, what have you got?" Enough woolgathering. It was time for business.

"The distributor found more parts that weren't ours packed in our boxes," he told him. "They've pulled our filters from the shelves and are shipping them back. They won't send out anymore filters from Blake Industries until this problem is all cleared up."

"Have you traced where the switch occurred?" Jonathan asked.

"Not yet."

"Have you contacted Damion yet?" Damion Hammond was the new chief of security at Blake Industries. Jonathan had hired him a year ago.

"He's doing a security check or whatever he does to protect us on our end. The distributor is checking its records to make sure the switch isn't occurring there."

"Good, the quicker we get this solved, the better."

"We've added extra checks here, too. Every shipment that goes out will be checked by trusted personnel that have been with Blake Industries more than ten years."

"Keep me posted," Jonathan told him. He slowly dropped the phone in the cradle.

Jonathan wasn't under any illusion that all of the good people of Nottoway thought of the company first and what its destruction would do to thousands of people employed there.

Living in an era of the get-rich-quick mentality where people didn't care who they hurt or why or how they acquired their ill-gotten gains had kept security companies increasing their business at an alarming rate. He was all for entrepreneurial activities as long as it was done through honesty.

He did what he could for the people of Nottoway. But nothing angered him more than anyone putting his company in jeopardy.

The meeting was near its end by the time a call was forwarded to Johanna at two. It was Jonathan. The other three people got up to take a break in the kitchen, stretch their arms and legs, and rotate their necks. Johanna went into the master bedroom and used the phone on the wall near the balcony door. She opened the French doors and walked onto the balcony that looked out on the river. Several people walked the paths. Some sat in iron lawn chairs that were placed underneath trees and near flower beds.

"Hello, Jonathan." Their relationship still hovered uncertainly, especially after the movie. Jonathan tried to reassure her about Sheryl, but they'd been unable to achieve their earlier ease.

"Wanna play hooky and leave work early today?" he asked her with a jovial air.

"Can't," she responded, "I've been in a meeting all day and I have some paperwork to complete before I leave. Then a trip to town to shop for a gift for Pam's oldest daughter."

"A birthday present."

"How did you . . . Mom," Johanna guessed.

"She invited me. I'm like one of the family," he mimicked Gladys' tone.

"You don't have to come, you know."

"Sure I do. I'm dating her daughter," he said. "Can't afford to get on her bad side."

Johanna remained silent.

"When are you going to town?" he asked.

"Around four."

"Mind if I tag along? I need to pick up a gift, too."

"Jonathan, she doesn't expect that of you." Johanna rubbed her forehead and leaned against the railing.

"I'll pick you up at four. The hotel or cabin?"

When she didn't respond, he said, "We need to talk."

Where was her willpower? "All right. The cabin." Hopefully, she'd have time for a quick shower and change of clothing before he arrived.

Walking back to join the meeting, everyone sat at the table with cups of coffee. "We can get Karina Dye's restaurant to do some of the catering. It's good to use some of the local businesses since the function will be way too large for our kitchens to prepare everything. It gives them a good feeling about our business." Johanna flipped through some pages. "Albert, her number is on page four of the handout."

"All right."

"And we've agreed the Higabothums will provide their homemade ice cream. You tested it last week, didn't you? What were your feelings?"

"The ice cream was delicious and they were charming," he said.

"Good. You can talk to them and work up a contract." Johanna went through her list. "The barbecue. Mrs. Drucilla prepares hogs for sale twice a year. Tylan actually does the work, but talk to her and see if she's willing to provide us with five for the opening. Our pit will only hold one. You can barbecue it and let it be a conversational piece. We'll slice that last.

"We're going to need everyone working that night. Even the employees who won't actually begin work until next month when the renovations are complete. We need measurements to send to the rental company for their clothing that night. Each department should send their list to Pam by Thursday."

Everyone nodded and made notes.

"Pamela, the invitations should be mailed by the end of this month. I chose the blue, but we have until the end of the week for the wording. I may want to make changes."

A cheer went up.

"You'd think those invitations were her first child the way she labored on them," Pam said.

Johanna realized the hotel was her baby.

The grand opening was going to be a gala affair.

Johanna leaned her head against the headrest of Jonathan's car and listened to the music as he drove to Petersburg.

The Woodrow Mall had lain vacant for several years until two years ago when a group of businessmen got together to reopen it, bringing some of the lost retail revenue and jobs back to Petersburg. Southpark Mall in Colonial Heights was much larger but many quaint upscale shops had purchased space in the Woodrow and it thrived. Victor Wallace, Karina's ex, had been one of the men on the deal.

They walked through the wide, well-lit corridor. The walls sparkled with fresh coats of white paint.

When they passed Paula's Boutique, Johanna made a mental note to stop there for fresh lingerie.

"Where are we going?" Jonathan asked her when they were halfway down the hall.

"The Jewelry Store. Nicole has a debutante ball coming up. I'm giving her a pearl necklace to wear."

"You'll spoil her."

"That's what aunts are for."

A saleslady helped them immediately upon their entrance, and lifted the necklace Johanna pointed to out of the glass case.

Johanna tried it on and Jonathan hooked the clasp. His warm hands caressing her neck lingered longer than they should have. Heat flooded Johanna and butterflies tumbled in her stomach as she stepped away from his touch while her treacherous body wanted to lean into him.

"They look gorgeous on you."

Johanna cleared her throat. "She'll like these, I think," she said.

Puzzled by his action, Johanna narrowed her eyes at him as he looked innocently on. Why the intimacy now when he always stopped their lovemaking?

Johanna twisted the necklace around using the mirror on the case to unclasp it herself as Jonathan talked to the saleslady.

He pointed to a diamond earring jacket.

"Do you think she'll like these?" he asked.

"She'll love them, but it's too much."

"Not too much for a debutante." He held them to her ears and asked the saleslady for pearl studs, which she quickly handed to him.

"Do you know what her ring size is?" he asked Johanna.

"Six and a half, the same as mine."

He pointed to an opal ring and asked Johanna to try it on. After he saw it on her finger, he settled on the earrings.

"I'll take these," he said. She can wear them with the necklace. "Could you wrap them?" he asked the saleslady.

"Of course," the woman replied and boxed the items in front of them.

Johanna smiled, as she boxed the earrings. "Nicole will fall in love with you."

"And what about you?" he asked as the saleslady wrapped the gifts at a distance.

The smile left Johanna's face as she watched him. "Is that what you want?" she whispered.

"Yes," He wasn't smiling. "I do."

"Jonathan . . . "

"I don't expect anything from you right now. It's just—you're special to me."

"Here you are," the saleslady interrupted.

They both jumped at the intrusion. Johanna handed her a check and Jonathan a platinum Visa.

Johanna pondered his statement as they waited for their receipts.

"Nicole will be so pleased. I usually give the children five shares of some stock on their birthday with a toy for the younger ones or a trinket for Nicole."

"You're passing on the tradition from Smith."

"It was the best thing he's ever done for me. I want it to become a family tradition."

The saleslady handed them receipts and they left with their packages.

"Where to next?" Jonathan asked once they left the store.

"I need to go by Paula's."

"I'll pick up dinner while you shop. An Ethiopian restaurant opened up a few months ago in the mall."

"I love Ethiopian food."

Johanna ran into Paula's boutique. The tall, slim woman greeted her immediately.

"As I live and breathe. I was wondering when you'd get by here," she said. "Your hotel is the hottest news for fifty miles."

The ladies hugged. They'd been friends in high school.

"You knew I'd have to come by sooner or later. I need lingerie," Johanna said.

"For what occasion?" she asked naughtily.

"I want something sexy. A woman always wants to feel good about herself." Shopping in Paula's was a treat. She'd moved from a downtown location to the mall a year ago. The store still had plenty of room.

"Say no more."

Paula led her down an aisle, passing racks of dresses, pants, blouses and coats to get to the back of the store. Several tables and racks of lingerie occupied the area. Bright light illuminated the array of bras, teddies, garter belts, and bikini underwear. Something for every woman's taste. Johanna selected several sets of underwear and two nightgowns before meeting Jonathan at the restaurant. Opting to wear one set, she'd torn the tags off them to take to the register. She wondered if she looked as naughty as she felt. Leaving everything up to Jonathan was getting her nowhere.

If Jonathan seriously sought her affection, tonight,

he'd see her as more than his sister's best friend, a businesswoman or someone comfortable to talk with. If he stopped this time, she'd never forgive him.

Jonathan drove directly to his house when they left town.

Once there, Johanna dialed her cabin and got her messages off the machine. One was from her mom. From past experience, Johanna knew that if she didn't call Gladys, her mom would be at her cabin before the night was over, or send Emmanuel. She didn't know which was worse.

"Hi Dad. I was calling Mom. She left a message on my answering machine."

"She's out. Went grocery shopping for some last-minute things for Wednesday night. She's due back anytime."

"Could you tell her I'll call tomorrow?"

He paused and Johanna heard voices in the background. "She just walked in. Hold on a minute," her father said.

Johanna waited for her mom to come to the phone.

"Hi Johanna," Gladys greeted. "I don't need anything now. Thought I'd get you to take me to town. But Emmanuel took me instead."

"Good. Well, I'll see you Wednesday, okay?"

"Okay, baby. Get Jonathan to pick you up."

Johanna chuckled at her mom's one-track mind. "All right."

"The table is set," Jonathan said from across the room, indicating the cocktail table.

"I'm starved." Johanna went to the bathroom to wash her hands. She felt naughty wearing a thong. She'd never had the inclination to wear one before. The unusual cut made it impossible to forget that she was wearing it. A smile lit her face as she thought of Jonathan's reaction when he saw it.

They sat on the floor in front of the couch. "Umm. What did you get?"

"Mild and spicy to suit any taste."

Tearing a piece of Ethiopian bread, Johanna used it to break off a piece of spicy chicken and fed it to Jonathan.

His eyes widened at the gesture. He caught her hand with his own and licked her fingers.

Johanna hoped he'd started down a path he wanted to go. He'd said he cared for her and wanted her to love him and hoped it was true.

Then, his hands were at her lips, holding bread and meat between his fingers. She opened her mouth to his offering. They fed each other throughout the meal, taking and giving, until after only eating a quarter of his dinner, Jonathan scooted closer to her and pressed his mouth to hers.

Her mouth opened to his hot and insistent tongue.

He glanced at her and she turned her lips to his neck and kissed him there. He smelled clean with a touch of woodsy cologne. His arms wrapped around her and he took his finger and tilted her chin. It seemed an eternity of anticipation before his lips touched hers.

She lifted her arms around his neck, lazily caressing his ear and easing a finger in his collar.

"Umm," Jonathan moaned against her lips.

"We're just getting started." She reached her hands under his shirt, lifted it over his head and raked her fingers through the dark hairs on his chest.

"Are you sure you're ready for this?" he asked her, his voice rough and needy.

"I've never been more sure of anything." She gazed at him, her heart thumping against her chest. "Are you sure?"

He searched her face, his eyes piercing and direct.

Leaning against her, he pressed her against the seat of the couch. "I'm sure," he said. The kiss wasn't leisurely this time. It was deep, hot and thorough, carrying her on a tidal wave. His hands trailed her thigh, touching her, caressing her, driving her wild with need. He lifted himself from her, his breath ragged.

Gazing in her eyes, he unsnapped her jeans, touching her as he slid her zipper down. His touch was exquisite against her skin. Then he lifted her sweater over her head, caressing her. His eyes opened wider when he saw her lacy mauve bra that left little to his imagination.

She reached down, and unzipped his jeans. He sat up, waiting for her next move. Johanna sat up and unsnapped his jeans. Reaching inside, she stroked the length of him. He was as well endowed in his pants as he was everywhere else.

She rose, held her breath and made sure he got the back view of her before sliding her pants down her legs inch by inch and stepping out of them.

Abruptly, he caught her around her waist, startling a laugh out of her and dragged her back, kissed her hip exposed by the thong she wore. This wouldn't be the last time she'd wear a thong. He turned her and ran his tongue along her abdomen, his hands splaying her hips. "Do you wear thongs and lacy see-through bras sitting in those meetings every day?" he asked, his voice husky with desire.

"This package was gift-wrapped just for you." She ran her hands along his shoulders, stroking the rippling muscles there.

He stood, swooped her in his strong arms and carried her to his bedroom, laying her on the center of his emerald spread. There would definitely be no stopping this time.

Kneeling, he lifted her foot in his hand, kissed the instep, sending a hailstorm of flutters through her. Time stood still as he stroked, kissed, and licked every inch of her until she pushed him on his back and enjoyed the texture of his body. She touched, kneaded, and kissed muscle after muscle, his deep masculine groans serenading her until neither of them could stand to wait another moment.

He rolled her over, shielded himself with a prophylactic and slowly entered her. When her softness completely enclosed him, he stilled, letting her bask in his length before he moved in the cadence as old as time, rocking, pulsing, touching, to carry her to the crest of desire and over the mountain peak, then quickly followed her culmination.

Her arms strained as she circled his back, her legs trembled as they encased his hips between them until the pulsating ceased and they fell limp.

CHAPTER 9

"Surprise!" everyone shouted out as Nicole entered the house.

Her sparkling brown eyes lit up, her hands automatically flying to her cheeks. "Oh, my." Embarrassment warred with pleasure as she advanced into the small kitchen that was packed with family and Jonathan.

"Happy birthday, granddaughter." Gladys plopped the platter of fried chicken on the table and captured her granddaughter in her plump arms, crushing the corsage Nicole wore on her blue blouse.

"Let her get some air, Gladys," Henry called out, waiting his turn.

Her grandmother let her go, dabbing at her eyes. She always got teary-eyed at family gatherings.

The corsage lay crushed against Nicole's chest, but no one mentioned the perfidy as her grandfather gathered her within his strong arms.

Johanna helped her mother carry platter after platter of food into the dining room, the event reminding her of her own homecoming less than a month ago. Had it only been a month since she'd returned? She felt like she'd been here forever. Jonathan had a great deal to do with that.

The fight among the children ensued, just as last time, and this time, again James had to intervene. But Uncle Emmanuel easily solved the problem with the seating. He plopped Anthony and Monica on either side of him.

The baby focused on the gifts piled in a corner of the dining room. After slyly watching until his mother's attention was elsewhere, he went to investigate.

Johanna snagged him up just as he started to tear into a package decorated with bright wrapping paper. "No you don't, you little tiger." She nuzzled his cheek with her lips and tickled his tummy, immediately throwing him into a giggling fit. When she stopped, he asked for more.

Then she caught sight of Jonathan watching her, and wondered at his thoughtful expression.

When she cocked her head to the side and raised an eyebrow, he merely smiled at her.

Business had intervened after their night of love-making, leaving her uncertain of his feelings and thoughts. None of her other relationships captured her heart as Jonathan had done. Perhaps the special kinship she and Jonathan always shared prevented her from totally focusing on other men. And perhaps she measured other men by his qualities that she found so appealing.

In other men, some element was always missing; the inability to communicate well, irritating habits, the incapability to form that bond she desired, but most of all, that special elusive link had never materialized to make her believe that that person was the one she could spend her life with and would never tire of him—until Jonathan.

Even with Jonathan, she must take care that his bond with Sheryl wasn't so strong that he couldn't love another.

Johanna knew she couldn't compete with the memories of a dead woman.

After everyone was so stuffed with dinner they could barely move, Nicole pulled Johanna aside.

With trepidation and with no one to monitor Gladys, Johanna left Jonathan in her mother's care, hoping she and Nicole would stay close enough to them to eavesdrop and to intervene if necessary.

Nicole had other ideas. Johanna barely had time to drop the dish towel into Emmauel's hand as she was dragged outside into the night.

"Aunt Johanna?" Nicole asked cautiously, twisting the ring her mom had given her around and around on her finger.

Johanna caught the teenager's hand in her own.

"Yes?" Johanna said in answer to her inquiry.

"The grand opening is going to be a big deal. I feel like it's part of history, you know?"

In the yard light, Nicole's eyes lit up as she talked to her aunt.

"Well," Johanna considered, letting go of Nicole's hand. "I never thought of it quite that way. But, I guess it is." She nodded her head.

"I . . . " She twisted the ring on her finger again. "I want to be a part of it all. I want to work and help during the opening." In the quiet, she said, "It's right after school closes so it won't interfere with my classes." She watched Johanna, anxiety clouding her wide, beautifully expressive eyes.

"What would you like to do?" Johanna asked her, trying to think of where she could use her or where Nicole could get the most out of the experience.

"I don't know. Maybe greet people." She shrugged her small shoulders.

"Let me think about it, all right? Perhaps you can work with me that night. Greet people, answer their questions about the hotel, hand out brochures," Johanna thought a moment. "Or perhaps you can monitor Patrick's exhibit."

In her excitement, Nicole clapped and almost knocked Johanna over when she hugged her. "I'm sorry," she said, tears misting her youthful eyes.

"I'm so pleased you're interested." Johanna brushed a stray wisp of hair back. "We'll think about it and come up with the perfect position for you. Furthermore, have you thought about a summer job?"

Nicole clasped her hand in front of her, her eyes growing big. "Would you . . . would you let me work at the hotel?" The excitement in the teenager's face and her enthusiasm reminded Johanna of herself at that age.

"Of course. What's the point of being the owner's niece if you can't get some privileges?"

Johanna almost toppled again under Nicole's youthful exuberance.

Squeezing Johanna's neck, she said, "I didn't think you'd let me. I was so frightened to ask you."

"Never be afraid to ask for what you want when you're willing to put your best work into it, Nicole. Otherwise how will you accomplish your dreams?" She patted the younger girl's back.

"Thank you, Auntie. I love you." She'd reverted back to the name she'd called Johanna as a child.

"Oh, honey. I love you, too." Johanna reflected

that children could tear your heart apart one moment, but the next they sent you soaring to the sky.

To get some uninterrupted time to work, Johanna left the hotel at eleven to work in her cabin for a few hours. Soon after, her niece, Monica, called and asked if she and Kara, Karina's daughter, could stay with her. They would be "as quiet as mice," she assured Johanna.

Johanna agreed.

"I have plenty of food in the refrigerator. You can play on the deck."

"Can we try your makeup?" they asked with hopeful expressions on their faces.

Remembering the Avon samples she'd been given and the makeup she'd purchased that didn't suit her was stashed in a drawer, Johanna trouped into the bedroom, pulled it out and handed the whole bag to them.

"Help yourselves." She and Karina had hours of fun experimenting with makeup as teenagers. Jonathan would give Karina money and they'd buy to their hearts' content. Johanna laughed at the memories of their foolishness. But they were fond memories.

Then she recalled the time when, to her horror, Jonathan had walked in on them and stopped dead in his tracks, checked his expression, turned his back with his shoulders suspiciously shaking, and told them to be sure they washed it off before they left the house.

Johanna had tried to look grown up, thinking maybe he would notice her, but she was too young to overtly pursue him. He'd never ridiculed them, but Johanna sensed his stifled amusement. Thoroughly mortified, it had been years before she'd experimented with makeup again. Thinking back, she probably looked like a clown. She and Karina had applied enormous amounts of makeup with a heavy hand.

With the children suitably occupied, Johanna concentrated on her computer files of names and companies she'd worked with and recorded over the past ten years, who would receive invitations to the opening and who had meetings small enough to use her hotel facilities.

They'd done well with bookings for the summer schedule, but companies and associations needed a reminder that space was available for the fall, winter and spring of next year.

With all the amenities the Nottoway Inn had to offer, it indeed was the accommodations they sought.

Two hours later, a knock sounded at the outer door. Wondering why the children didn't answer it, Johanna left her desk and padded to the door and opened it to Patrick.

"I'm glad you came." She moved aside, giving him room to pass. "Have a seat."

"I'll only be a minute. I got your message on the answering machine and was in the neighborhood," he told her. He'd probably driven right over.

"You're going to need a seat for this news," Johanna told him.

"What is it?" he asked, concern written all over his brown face.

"It's good news. Don't worry," she told him, patting him on the arm. "Come on, sit down."

Sitting on the edge of the sofa cushion, he gave her his undivided attention.

"I was thinking of adding a unique twist to the grand opening. Although several of your pieces are already displayed in the hotel, I was thinking of the many pieces you have finished in your studio. If you agree, we can feature an art show for you. We can set one of the conference rooms aside as a gallery."

Patrick slumped back on the couch, working his mouth, but unable to utter one word.

Johanna laughed. "Well?" she asked. "Do you agree or not," she teased. "Are you telling me you don't want the hotel to showcase your work?" She laughed at his comical expression.

"I . . ." He closed his mouth and tried again. "I've got tons of pieces you can use."

"Great, because I just received confirmation that a curator I met two years ago has agreed to come and view your work. Have you heard of John Delacort? He has a museum in New York."

Jumping up, almost hitting the ceiling, Patrick whooped and bellowed. He picked Johanna up, twirled her around, almost tripping over a footstool, then dumped her back on a chair.

Johanna's ears rang so that she didn't hear the clatter of the children clamoring into the kitchen from the deck to investigate the commotion.

"What's going on?" they yelled.

Laughing, it took a moment for Johanna to answer them. "Patrick just got some good news."

"Some very good news," he shouted.

Running and jumping through the great room, shouting "yes" and other assorted mumbled words, he reminded Johanna of when she was a child and Mrs. Drucilla's chickens were running around with their heads cut off.

The girls hovered together, keeping a safe distance, puzzled at the commotion.

"He really is all right," Johanna assured them. "Good news tends to unsettle people sometimes."

The shouting and exuberance continued for

another three minutes before Patrick brought himself under control. Then Johanna got a look at the girls' faces for the first time. Unfortunately, so did Patrick.

"You all practicing early for Halloween this year?" he asked them.

Johanna could have hit him for his insensitivity. He didn't have sisters, so she understood.

With mortified looks on their faces, the girls quickly turned and eased out the side door.

"Patrick!" Johanna admonished.

"What did I do?" was his innocent reply.

"The fact that you had no sisters is the only thing saving me from blistering your ears this very moment. And the fact that you're so happy."

"They were playing, weren't they?"

"They are teenagers, Patrick."

"I thought they were . . . " he stopped, gave her a helpless look. "Were they serious?"

"Of course they were, you dunce."

"Well, how was I supposed to know that?" he asked, glancing cautiously toward the deck. "All right, all right." He threw up his hands at her censuring glare. "I'll make it up to them, somehow."

Marching through the kitchen, he slid the door open. "Hey, I was just kidding, you two. You look kinda good," Johanna heard. "All grown up looking. Your dad's gonna have to beat the boys off with a stick."

With him layering it on so thick, Johanna called him back inside. "They don't believe a word you said," she informed him once he returned.

He shrugged his shoulders. "I don't know what to say to girls that age. They look like clowns," he mumbled under his breath and looked toward the deck to make sure they didn't overhear.

Johanna shook her head. "Girls are very sensitive at this age. You should encourage them."

"Okay. After what you've done for me, I'll do anything you tell me to."

"On a serious note, I have to give my final edit to the printer tomorrow. I need a commitment if we are going to show your work at the opening."

"I'm committed. The house is filled with pieces. I just finished a few new ones I think you'll like." He sat on the couch. "Johanna, how will I ever thank you for this. Do you think he'll think my art's good enough?" Unable to stay still, Patrick jumped up to pace.

"You're going to be famous. The *Dispatch* ran an article in the Art section on your sculptures. They wouldn't have if they thought your art was unworthy. Don't worry." She patted his hand when he neared her.

"Are you kidding? I'll do nothing but worry." He resumed his pacing. "I'm working on one piece now. I'll try to finish it for the show." He faced Johanna.

"Thank you," he whispered, lips trembling. He headed for the door, a suspicious wetness gleaming in his eyes.

Johanna sighed and rose. She'd talk to the girls and maybe tell them of her first experience with makeup, hoping it would lift their spirits. Before she made it to the deck, the door rattled with another knock.

She switched directions to answer it.

Smith stood with his usual harassed expression creasing his brows. "Gal, you been working." He held his fishing hat, resplendent with tassels, in his hands, turning it. His chambray shirt was covered by a tan fishing vest.

"What are you doing here?" Johanna asked.

"Had to come see what I could do about this mess. I haven't been home yet." He stepped into the room, glancing around.

"You should have let me know. I'd have had the house cleaned for you. It should be fine, though. I sent someone over two weeks ago," she said. "It may need a little dusting."

Smith had handed her a key to the place the morning he'd left.

"A little dust never bothered me. I'm going to start dragging out boxes, see what I can find," he said.

"Have a seat," Johanna said.

He shook his head, no. "I'll just be a minute."

"Do you think you have documents about your uncle?"

He shrugged his shoulders. "We'll see."

"Thank you, Smith. I appreciate your coming back." She squeezed his arm. "Come over and have dinner with me tonight, all right?"

He waved a hand and shook his head. "I'm not for all that fancy food. Turns a man's stomach."

"We've got plain fare, too. Something to suit everybody's tastes," Johanna assured him.

"I'll think about it." He eased out the door.

"Do come. Maybe Jonathan will join us."

"I'll call you," he called out. Opening the door to his truck, he scooted Travis over and climbed in. "I really want to know if I have a cousin and why he never contacted me before." He closed the door with a snap and started up the motor.

Johanna waved as he backed out of her drive. He'd waited anxiously for years to move to Florida, and now he was back because of her. Missing his fishing. Hopefully he'd take some time away from his search to enjoy his favorite pastime. If this man was a relative, why didn't he contact Smith?

Before Johanna could close the door, the telephone rang. She may as well have stayed at the hotel for all the work she was getting done. She picked up the receiver.

"I haven't been able to concentrate on work all day from thinking of that thong." She was instantly mollified at hearing Jonathan's voice.

"It's been difficult for me, too."

"What time are you getting off today?" he asked.

"The usual time. But Smith's returned from Florida to search through family papers for me. I promised him dinner. Want to join us?"

He groaned. "Let's make it early. I need you to myself tonight."

She'd get Pam to pick up the kids early. "Hold that thought. Dinner won't last long."

"I'm finding I'm a selfish man. I don't like to share you."

"I can live with that." Johanna twirled the phone cord around her finger.

"What did you have for lunch?"

"I haven't yet."

"Why don't I join you." His voice sent electrical shocks through her.

"I'd love that." Then she remembered the kids. "I've got Monica and Kara."

"I'm keeping them this afternoon. I promised to take them and the boys fishing," he said. "I'll pick up something and talk them into taking a walk—a long walk."

His seductive pitch fluttered through her.

"It'll take me just a few minutes to get there."

The receiver almost slid out of Johanna's hand. "We'll be waiting."

Twenty minutes later, Jonathan stood with his hand on the doorjamb, tall and graceful, full of quick energy and looking too good for the middle of the day in his three-piece business suit. Johanna wanted to slide that jacket right off his shoulders to feel the strength beneath.

"Hi," she said instead, a little self-conscious after last night.

He didn't mutter a word as he approached her, his expression serious, his gaze unswerving. With one smooth motion, he shut the door behind him, reached out and tugged her into his arms. Leaning against the door, his lips crushed hers as he pressed her against his long length.

Johanna slid her hand under his jacket, feeling the smooth texture of his vest, wanting the hot texture of his skin.

He lifted his head, parting his lips from hers. "Hello," he said, his voice throaty, the whisper of his breath caressing her face.

Wow! she thought. "What a greeting!" she muttered against his lips.

"I've barely gotten any work done from thinking about you all morning."

Johanna smiled at him. She'd tossed in restless sleep after he delivered her at her cottage last night, wishing she could break that proper reserve he held so dear.

"Come on. If we don't eat lunch, we're going to shock the kids."

"If only," she sighed.

"Just hold that thought until tonight," he said nuzzling her neck. "I called the restaurant from my office. They'll deliver our lunch any minute."

* * *

Johanna had dinner delivered to her cottage. She and Smith ate on the deck facing the river. The day was warm, but not hot, sending a light, warm breeze across the water.

Smith looked much more relaxed than when he'd left Nottoway. He still wore his usual gear of fishing hat and vest. Johanna didn't know when she'd actually seen him without his uniform.

When he arrived, he'd brought a heavy-bound volume that looked like an old Bible with him. He'd placed it on her coffee table before they went outside to enjoy the early evening by the river.

Johanna set the table with steaming meat loaf, potatoes, asparagus and her mother's hot fluffy biscuits—his favorites—and country fresh homemade lemonade.

He moaned and rubbed his stomach when he saw the fare. "I haven't eaten this well since I left," he said.

"How are you enjoying Florida?" Johanna asked, after they started their meal. The rushing water on the river was a trusted friend that she enjoyed. She hoped he felt the same way. Now and then, guests would pass by, walking along the shore. But not many ventured that far up.

"Found some good fishing holes," he said. "Been looking at the family Bible where they recorded everybody's birthday and death. There's nothing on Samuel."

"Maybe your uncle Raymond had a child he never told you about."

"Not likely. Raymond never did anything with the hotel. He was kinda wild, you know." Smith ate a bite of meat loaf.

"Raymond stayed in trouble and Dad kept paying money to get him out. Never did have much left to spend on the hotel. The Depression nearly cleaned the family out. Then Raymond managed to wipe out the rest. The only thing left was the hotel.''

"Did he ever marry?"

"No."

What worried Johanna most was what would happen if this man was Smith's cousin and refused the settlement from the insurance company. What if he demanded to hold ownership of half the hotel? What consideration would she get for the money and time she'd already invested?

Sometimes family Bibles didn't include family secrets. Johanna pondered what web of secrecy surrounded the Smith family?

Several cars were parked in Jonathan's yard when Johanna arrived around eight-thirty. She recognized Pam's and Karina's car, but not the others. Johanna parked her car under a tree.

Exiting the vehicle, she heard children's excited voices in the backyard and smelled cooking from a grill. Jonathan was probably grilling hot dogs and hamburgers for the children.

She walked along the row of hedges that led to the back of the house. Under the dull haze of the patio light sat a bevy of guests.

"Aunt Johanna," Monica called out.

Monica took Johanna's hand, swinging it back and forth as they approached the patio.

Phoenix Dye stood and approached her. "You finally made it home."

"How are you?" she asked.

"Couldn't be better," he said, a twinkle in his eye.

"All right, what's up?" Johanna asked, knowing more than her presence made him especially giddy.

Phoenix had lived in Alexandria when he was an FBI special agent.

"I'm going to be a dad again," he said.

"Oh, Phoenix," Johanna hugged him. "Congratulations. Three again."

"It's only one this time. We checked," Karina, came up beside him."

"I'm so happy for you," Johanna said.

"This big lug is happy, too. You'd think I delivered him the moon."

"A baby is even better. How do the triplets feel about this?" she asked as Pam, Tylan and his wife, Clarice, approached them.

"They're ecstatic."

"Johanna, you remember Clarice, don't you?" he said of the beautiful woman fighting with a wet nap to wipe mustard off a wiggling two-year-old.

"I do, hello," Johanna said.

"Hi." Clarice was interrupted when Kara and Monica came for the baby, who eagerly climbed out of his mother's arms to join the fun.

"Where's Jonathan and James?" Johanna finally asked.

"They're closeted away in a meeting upstairs in the den. They've been there since we arrived. We're about to send in food, but no one is brave enough to approach them. You've been elected to do so. Jonathan wouldn't dare bark at you," Karina said.

"He hasn't had dinner yet?"

"Nope." Karina retrieved two plates, each heaping with a hamburger, hot dog, potato salad and baked beans.

Johanna secured the strap to her purse on her shoulder and took the plates. "Lead the way," she said.

Karina opened the French doors for her. "They're in the den."

Johanna climbed the stairs to the second floor. The door was closed. "Knock, knock," she called out.

She heard footsteps approaching before the door snapped open. A harassed expression coated Jonathan's face until he saw her. He immediately reached for the plates. "Hi, sweetheart. You're a sight for sore eyes."

Bending, he planted a quick kiss on her lips.

"Hi," she said softly. At the clearing of a throat, Johanna glanced across the room. "Oh, hi James."

"Hello, Johanna. This man is a workhorse. Thank you for thinking of this starving soul."

"Actually, I was coerced. You frightened everyone away. They sacrificed me to the lion's den."

"I'm that bad, hmm?" Jonathan said.

"Afraid so. I'm going to let you get back to business. What can I get you to drink?"

"Anything, for me," James said. "I'm parched."

"And you?" She glanced at Jonathan, her tone softening.

"I've got the drinks right here," Karina said from the doorway. "Is it safe to enter?"

"Barely," Johanna remarked.

"I'll be quick." She handed the drinks to the men and disappeared.

CHAPTER 10

Silence was bliss after a harried, noisy crowd, Johanna thought, lifting her hand to stroke Jonathan's face later that night. She shifted inch by inch on the living room couch, trying not to disturb Jonathan's rest.

The boys slept peacefully downstairs in the only bedroom with twin beds. Kara was spending the night with Monica. The girls had quickly become fast friends.

Jonathan had fallen asleep, his head on her lap. Business intruded and extended the day into forever, it seemed. Instead of enjoying the evening with his niece and nephews, Jonathan had been closeted in a meeting with James until everyone had dispersed. He'd been left with a splitting headache.

After, Johanna had urged the boys to dress for bed and she and Jonathan had retired to the upstairs living room. She'd turned on the quiet soul music and it had immediately put Jonathan to sleep.

She should get up and leave, but she loathed to disturb him while he slept so peacefully. Even now, he hadn't totally relaxed.

She'd like nothing more than to curl up in his king-size bed snuggled in his arms, but with the boys sleeping in the room next to his, she couldn't spend the night.

Jonathan turned on his side, facing her, but he continued to sleep.

Leaning toward the side table, she flipped the switch on the lamp, enfolding them in darkness. It took several minutes for her eyes to adjust to it and soon light from the halogen lamp in the yard filtered around the shades.

She'd leave in a few minutes, but for now she'd listen to the music and rest.

The sorrowful love songs of Aretha Franklin prompted her thoughts to return to her relationship with Jonathan. What kind of relationship did they share? What did he expect from it? What did she expect from him? And where did she want them to go from here?

Since college, she'd been so career-driven, that she'd never considered marriage, though she'd dated. But Jonathan was her idol—the man who'd touched her heart in a special way. He was also the man who'd loved Sheryl so intensely that it had taken him years to get over her, if he were over her even now. What she'd give for Jonathan to love her the way he had loved Sheryl all those years ago.

Glancing down at him, she ran her hand lightly over his face. Instinctively, he turned his face toward her hand and kissed her palm.

Just a few more minutes and then she'd leave, Johanna promised herself as she settled more comfortably on the seat cushion. Slowly, she continued to run her hand softly over Jonathan's shoulders, the same soft caress that had eased him into sleep half an hour ago.

Aretha Franklin belted out a tune from the old Motown compilation CD in the machine. Music that should have been soothing to the soul had the opposite effect. Instead, it left her troubled.

Before long, Johanna's eyelids felt heavy, but she kept them open. Just a few more moments and she'd leave.

It was 2:00 A.M. when Johanna awakened. She stretched, surprised that she'd actually fallen asleep. Slowly easing her hips from under Jonathan's head, she stood and stretched. As quiet as she was, Jonathan awakened anyway.

"Go back to sleep. You were so tired," she whispered.

He glanced at the clock across the room and quickly sat up. "I wasn't very good company, was I?" he said as he stifled a yawn.

"We don't always have to do something," she told him. "Do you feel more refreshed now?"

He nodded his head and rubbed a hand across his tired face.

"Why don't you go to bed, I'm going to the cabin after I get my purse from your room."

"At two in the morning?"

"I can't stay the night with the children here. They see too much as it is."

He groaned. "I forgot they were here. Some uncle I'm turning out to be. I haven't spent any time with them. And I've neglected you."

"They had a ball last night. Believe me. I had to drag them inside for bed."

She padded over to him and kissed him lightly on the mouth. "You don't always have to entertain me." He captured her around her waist, pulled her down on top of him and kissed her—a long and thorough kiss.

"Just give me a minute," he whispered after. "Then I'll take you home."

Johanna stood and straightened her clothes.

"My car's right outside," she told him. Slowly she approached the stairs.

"I don't want you driving this late at night." Jonathan had followed her.

"I do it all the time, Jonathan. You can't leave the kids. I'll be all right." Johanna descended the stairs and took her purse out of his bedroom closet.

"Call me the minute you get home. Do you have your car phone on you?"

"Yes, I do. It's right here." She patted her purse. "Tucked safely away in my purse."

"Store my number in the save function so you can quickly reach me if you need to."

Sighing, Johanna rooted through her purse for the phone and entered his number. "All done." She kissed his cheek which needed a shave. "Satisfied now?"

After she made a quick trip to the powder room, Jonathan walked her to the car.

"Call me the minute you arrive," he said again just before he closed her car door.

"I will."

It was pitch dark out tonight. Not even a sliver of moon presented itself to relieve the stark countryside. Only the illumination from the yard light offered some relief, and that was quickly left behind once Johanna drove out of Jonathan's yard.

* * *

After seeing Johanna off, every vestige of sleep had left Jonathan. He inhaled the sharp night air and entered the bottom floor. Looking in on the boys, their bodies bunched under the covers, he determined them fast asleep.

He walked to the French doors to gaze out into the night, wondering what it was about Johanna that made him want to spend every spare moment with her.

He was well aware of her mother's drive to push Johanna toward him—toward marriage, but Johanna wouldn't make love to him to trap him. Still some lingering doubt from years gone by, made him cautious.

As a child, Mrs. Jones and Johanna never saw eye to eye and her mother could never push Johanna into anything she didn't want. Many a time, Mrs. Jones had thrown up her hands and sent Johanna to her father saying she'd completely washed her hands of her younger daughter.

Henry would shake his head and then he and his daughter would spend a few minutes together talking. Jonathan only hoped the determination still remained in her and that Johanna was with him because she really wanted to be—not because eligible men were scarce, or to fulfill her mother's dream of having a wealthy man.

Jonathan sighed. So much to ponder. But how he wished he could have tucked her in bed with him tonight and spent the night reminding her how much he enjoyed her company.

The bigger question was how would he ever know if she really loved him? Did he have to settle for blind faith? Could he have blind faith in a woman after Sheryl?

Even Jonathan's reserve didn't keep the desire for Johanna at bay.

The only illumination along the winding country road was the light beaming from the headlights of Johanna's car. In the darkness, the tall trees climbed like canyons along each side of her.

She wouldn't give up this country life for anything, she thought as she rounded another curve and her eyes caught a flash of light.

Johanna slowed, wondering if she were seeing one of the deer that so often frequented the surrounding forests. Often she watched quietly from the cabin window while they frolicked in the clearing or observed them as they drank water from the river's edge on dew-shrouded mornings.

But as she drew closer, she realized the light was from a flashlight, not the illumination from a deer's eye.

Wondering who would be walking so late at night on a deserted road, Johanna slowed to almost a crawl and flipped the electronic lock to make certain her doors were locked. She strained her neck and eyes to decipher the identity of the person. Two people suddenly slowed and glared at her as her headlights pinned them.

They were children.

Karlton and Karl. Karl was dripping wet and shivering, his arms wrapped around his thin body.

Karlton carried the flashlight in one hand and a plastic grocery bag in the other.

"What?" Johanna said and slammed on her brakes.

Putting the car in park and pressing the emergency brake, she opened the door and stood.

"What are you doing out here?" she asked them. Before they could answer, she said, "Get in the car. I'll get a blanket for you, Karl."

"We don't need a ride," Karlton assured her. "Uncle Jonathan's house is just up the road."

"We're on our way back to Uncle Jonathan's, now," Karl assured her.

"I'm not discussing this with you at two-thirty. Get in the car," Johanna demanded.

Only a twelve-year-old would believe an adult would leave them to walk a dark road this time of the morning.

Karina had written to her often about the triplets' escapades over the years. Johanna thought the woman had embellished the tales a bit. Now, she wondered.

The boys glanced at each other and walked slowly, dragging their feet toward the car. Johanna leaned in the open door and pressed the electronic lock to unlock the other doors, then pulled the trunk release. She rounded the car to the trunk and took out an old blanket she kept there, then she went to the passenger side where Karl waited by the door and handed the blanket to him.

He wrapped the blanket around himself and settled in the front seat.

Glancing at both of the boys to make sure they'd buckled their seatbelts, she rounded the car and got in. The smell of fish had already permeated the interior of the car.

"How did you get wet?" she asked, as she turned the heat to full blast.

"We went fishing and I fell in the river when my fish tried to get away," he explained.

"Do you realize how dangerous that was?"

"I can swim," he said as if that made their excursion all right.

"So can I. I could have rescued him if he needed it," Karlton assured her.

The thought of both the boys drowning sent Johanna's pressure to the ceiling. She struggled for calm, thanking heaven she didn't have any children.

"I didn't need rescuing. I can swim just as well as you can," Karl said.

"What if . . . ?" Johanna cut in, then stopped herself. "I'm going to let your uncle handle this."

Karl stirred in the blanket. "You don't have to tell him, do you?"

"You can just let us off at the road. We'll just go in and go back to bed."

She put the car in gear and drove off. "Yes, I do have to tell him."

Both boys mumbled something under their breaths.

"I assume you caught plenty of fish," she said and wondered if she'd ever get the fishy smell out her car.

"We wanted some fish for breakfast."

"Fishing at 2:00 A.M." Johanna looked sideways at Karl as he hovered in the blanket. "Your uncle will have plenty to say to you."

A small path, a trail actually, used for the hayrides should be close by, Johanna realized as she accelerated. She drove at a snail's pace to keep from missing it and almost passed it before she spotted the barely detectable path hidden by tall, thick trees that had grown freely for hundreds of years. Johanna pulled into the path and backed out into the road, turning the car around to return to Jonathan's house.

The silence in the car was so thick you could almost slice it with a knife.

In a few short minutes, they reached the house.

"All right, let's go," Johanna said as she switched off the ignition and exited the car. Seeing a dark shadow round the house brought a scream to her throat.

"What happened?" Jonathan asked before the scream emerged further than her mind.

Johanna inhaled to quiet her startled heartbeat before she could talk.

"I found Karl and Karlton walking down the road. Other than to tell you they went fishing, I'll let them explain why to you."

From the interior light, Johanna could see Jonathan's frown turn to anger.

"You have pillows tucked under your covers?" Jonathan asked.

Karlton cleared his throat. "Yes," he said, dancing from foot to foot.

Karl shed the blanket but Johanna ordered him to keep it around him.

"I'll pick it up later," she told him.

"Thanks," he said and sent a nervous glance in his uncle's direction.

"Get in front of me and march inside," Jonathan said, his voice taut and hard. When the boys did as bidden, he turned to Johanna. "Thanks for bringing them back."

"Sure. Good night," she said and sat in the car.

He came closer and leaned down to kiss her lightly before closing the door.

Jonathan watched as Johanna started the ignition and backed out of the drive. Only then did he turn to follow the boys' steps to the house.

Karlton was sitting on the sofa in the great room. Karl stood nearby, hovering in the blanket.

"Go get out of those wet clothes and take a hot shower, Karl. We'll talk when you return."

He glanced at Karlton who remained on the sofa and sniffed the air. "You need a shower too. Use my bath."

Karlton relaxed as he made a quick escape.

Jonathan took the fish and put the bag in the refrigerator. He'd promised the boys he'd go fishing with them that afternoon, but James had returned from his trip and they'd spent the evening discussing business. He'd let the boys down.

"Start talking," Jonathan demanded, his hands on his hips. The boys were again dressed in their pajamas and they sipped on the hot chocolate Jonathan had given them. Jonathan realized that was a treat, not punishment.

"We thought we'd catch fish for our breakfast tomorrow morning," Karl started.

"The way we'd discussed," Karlton said. He always knew just the right thing to say to twist Jonathan's gut. "We wanted to surprise you."

"Didn't I tell you we were going fishing tomorrow?" Jonathan roared.

"But you might need to discuss business again with Mr. Evans. Or spend time with Aunt Johanna."

Jonathan ignored the excuse. "You deliberately disobeyed me."

"You didn't say that we couldn't go fishing," Karlton pointed out.

"Don't try your skewed logic on me, young man."

Karlton glanced away from Jonathan's glare.

"You promised," Karl said quietly.

"And I apologized for having to change our plans, but have I ever broken a promise to you?"

The boys glanced at him and shook their heads. "No," they said simultaneously.

"And you knew going fishing alone in the middle of the night was forbidden," Jonathan thundered, still shaky from Karl's trip in the dark water. What if they'd drowned?

"Yes," they answered again.

Jonathan raked a hand through his hair. He spent so little time with them anymore, he hated to use part of it punishing them.

"Go to bed," he told them.

As they escaped to the bedroom, Jonathan decided he'd think of some punishment that could be applied on their parents' time, not his.

Johanna sipped breakfast tea on the deck the next morning while watching joggers canter along the shore. An early-morning phone call from her mother had her out of bed sooner than she'd anticipated. Gladys Jones had no respect for the luxury of sleeping in on Saturday mornings.

Within ten minutes, she'd stopped by Johanna's to deliver piping-hot buttered biscuits before she continued on to her charity drive. Johanna offered a donation in the form of a check to her mother's charity.

Johanna's willpower failed to keep her from slipping two of the biscuits onto a plate and slathering them with homemade apple butter. After licking the last crumb from her fingers, she needed to join the joggers. Already she felt a pound or two heavier since she returned to Nottoway.

She heard a car door slam and descended the steps to see who had arrived.

Mrs. Drucilla and Luke were nearing her door.

"Hello," she called out, "I'm on the deck."

"We heard about the troubles and wanted to help in some way."

The older couple walked with her to the deck.

"That was kind of you," Johanna said. She hadn't really expected help from anyone.

"Well, I remember Smith's brother."

Johanna motioned them to chairs.

"Could I get you some tea? My mother just left some hot fluffy biscuits or I can have something delivered from the restaurant."

"We've eaten," Mrs. Drucilla said, "but I'll have a cup of tea."

"I could use a spot of tea myself," Luke said. "You got some jam to go with those biscuits?" he asked.

"Is apple butter all right?"

"My favorite."

It took only a few minutes to arrange the items on a tray. As soon as she'd served them, Johanna took a seat.

"We came," Mrs. Drucilla continued, "because I remembered a conversation with my mother. You know she was a midwife."

"No, I didn't," Johanna said.

"Well, I remember her saying that Raymond couldn't have children."

"Oh, really?" Johanna asked.

"Seems he caught a bad case of the measles as a boy. She tended him, you know."

"I wonder who Samuel Smith is then?"

"I don't know. But you know they didn't always keep good records back then. Midwives were supposed to send the records to Richmond, but not all of them did. My mom did though. I had to help her fill out the papers sometimes."

"Thank you, Mrs. Drucilla."

Luke quietly sipped his tea and enjoyed his biscuits.

"You know the church recorded baptismal records. They wouldn't have anything about births though. Now, they may have wedding information. But then he may not have married in the church."

"That's true. He was reputed to be wild. He may not have attracted a church-going lady of that era."

"Hmmp. They made them frisky back then just like they do now," Mrs. Drucilla interjected and picked up one of the biscuits from the serving platter.

Johanna made a mental note to pass the information on to her lawyer.

CHAPTER 11

Johanna wondered if Jonathan would visit her that evening. He was probably holed up in a stuffy office with James.

She'd worked at her own desk most of the day, but now she dressed with plans to mingle among the guests at the pig picking buffet.

A hog roast wasn't formal dining so, she chose to wear a dark gray pantsuit with a mauve blouse and flats. Pearl earrings and necklace completed the outfit.

It only took a minute to drive to the hotel, and by the time she made it to the barbecue, adults and children alike surrounded the pit. For effect, Albert had left the pig's head on and stuck an apple in its mouth. The heat from the pit warmed the cool air to just the right temperature.

The mayor and his wife were there as were a few of the Nottoway locals. Johanna didn't relish a conversation with Tina and her discourse on Sheryl. How would Tina feel if she was regularly slapped in the face with her husband's ex-girlfriend? Some people talked so much, they didn't think about the consequences of their conversations. But Johanna couldn't avoid them the entire evening. After all, the woman's husband did hold the most prominent political post in Nottoway.

Even now, they worked the crowd as thoroughly as they would at a fund-raiser, forgetting that the out-of-town guests could care less about their social position.

"Good evening, Tina, Mayor." Johanna spoke to them when they finally fell into her path.

"Oh, Johanna. I haven't attended a roast in I don't know how long," Tina told her.

"You've come up with a winner," Warren said, scanning the crowd.

"I'm glad you find it to your liking." Johanna tried not to look at the dab of barbecue sauce on the mayor's tie. He wasn't the neatest of men and she wondered how he and the fastidious Tina got along. Not one speck of anything had landed on Tina's green suit.

"Very much so," Tina said, craning her neck to look behind Johanna.

"A fine group of people," the mayor said. He sidled closer to Johanna. "See the couple at the table in the corner?"

Johanna discreetly looked in the direction he indicated.

"The one with the two children?" He all but pointed to Johanna's left.

As Tina sidled up to a smart-looking couple and started a conversation, Johanna sneaked a side view of a man with his hair combed to the side to cover a bald spot and a smartly dressed woman who she guessed took the three requisite trips to the health spa each week.

"I see them," she told him.

The man sitting in the corner behind the couple really caught her attention. There was a slick sneaky air about him that made her want to take another shower.

"He's campaign manager for Congressman Isle of Rhode Island. Gave me some good pointers for my own campaign next election." He dug a business card out his pocket for her to see.

Johanna nodded. "That's good," she told him.

"I think I'm going to try out some of his strategies. It's good to stay up to date."

Since he had no competition, Johanna speculated on what use he'd have for the advice.

Shoving the card back into place, he looked to the side. "And see the couple that look to be in their sixties over to your right?"

Johanna inclined her head in acknowledgment as she noticed the man with a deep tan and hulking muscles.

"He owns a chain of health clubs in Michigan. He and his wife thought this would be a good stop on their drive to Florida," he said, pleased he was hob-nobbing with the rich and famous beyond Nottoway. "We're going to play a round of golf together tomorrow morning."

"I see."

"You know, it wouldn't be a bad idea to open a health club here."

"Do you think it would survive? There's plenty of open spaces for people to walk and jog here."

"Health clubs are the rage now. Nottoway has got to keep current."

Johanna nodded a noncommittal reply, seeking

some way to divest herself of him as she saw Tina wave frantically at her husband.

"I think Tina's summoning you?"

A sick feeling dropped to the pit of Johanna's stomach when she saw Tina latch on to someone else.

Johanna hoped she didn't lose business when the word spread that the mayor of Nottoway made a pest of himself at hotel functions.

He glanced at his wife. "Well, enjoy your evening," he said as if he were the host instead of she.

Johanna watched him join the couple Tina had captured. What could one really do about nuisance politicians?

She continued to mingle among the guests, but tried not to be intrusive, since Tina and her husband had that department cornered.

The man in the corner hadn't moved. He watched the crowd as he slowly ate. Johanna had felt the hairs rise on the back of her neck and looked in his direction. This time she caught him gazing at her. Why?

After an hour, Johanna started to leave when the stranger beckoned her.

"Good evening, Ms. Jones." He extended a hand. He wore several large gold and diamond rings on his fingers. The navy-blue dress slacks, a white silk shirt and navy double-breasted jacket with a handkerchief in his pocket looked out of place with the jeans and jogging suits the other guests wore.

"Good evening," Johanna said, returning his oily handshake.

"Your resort is a virtual showplace." The smile he delivered didn't reach his eyes.

Something about him sent chills up Johanna's spine, but she dutifully thanked him. He reminded her of a pimp.

They were in a secluded area. Most of the guests

had finished their dinners and only a few stragglers remained behind to finish off the last of the barbecue.

"I thought that we should talk face to face." He straightened his tie, twisting his neck to the side.

"Oh? About what?" Johanna asked.

"Let me introduce myself. I'm Samuel Smith."

"I see," Johanna said, anger seeping through her.

"I think insurance companies and lawyers can be . . ." he paused as if searching for a word, "pesky inconveniences." He sniffed and rubbed the bridge of his nose. "I thought that you're a reasonable woman—an intelligent woman—and since half of the hotel, by right, is due me from my father's inheritance, we should be able to come to some equitable agreement." He pierced her with his gaze as he waited for her reply.

"And what terms did you have in mind, Mr. Smith?" Johanna crossed her arms underneath her breasts, wanting to strike out at the weasel.

"The hotel is quite a huge undertaking. But there's still plenty more to do. Why don't we, let's say, begin to work together?"

The rings flashed as he gestured with his hands. "Court cases cost a fortune. By the time we pay the lawyers we'd have to take out huge loans just to pay them off. It will be better for all concerned if we can come up with an agreement on our own." He picked an imaginary piece of lint off his suit and looked at her awaiting a response—as if he actually expected an immediate answer.

Johanna barely kept her anger in check. "You're mistaken, Mr. Smith," she told him. "It may cost you a fortune but I don't have to pay a dime for the court case." She lowered her arms to her side. "In the future, contact my lawyer if you wish to talk about business. I won't come to any terms with you."

Johanna presented her back to him and walked toward the door.

"You're going to have to deal with me sooner or later, you know," she heard him say. "I'm a patient man. I can wait." His threat hovered in the air.

Johanna paused. "Have you spoken to your uncle, Mr. Smith? Your only living relative on your father's side of the family?" She didn't wait for a reply, simply turned and continued on her course.

Of course he can wait, she thought. He'd waited all these years to issue a claim. What was one or two more?

Johanna passed Darlene Thompson on her exit and allowed only a few seconds to contemplate how much of their conversation the nosy woman had overheard. Johanna walked through the door and closed it, shutting out his sick rambling, wishing she could shut out his threat.

The slick weasel! He let her pay a fortune to refurbish the hotel and thought she'd actually consent to sharing her hard work with him when he'd done nothing to earn it. Just like a user. It'll be a cold day in hades when she'd come to any terms with him.

Johanna marched to her car and slammed the door. Starting the motor, she roared up the path to her cabin. She prayed Smith would find something to help her case.

With quick strides, Damion Hammond left Jonathan's office and shut the door soundlessly behind him.

Jonathan looked after him and thought he could know that man for a hundred years and still not truly get to know him. Damion had a nose for finding secrets.

"Do you think Tri-Parts is sabotaging us because we refused to consider their merger?" James asked from his seat across from Jonathan.

"It's a possibility. Damion will look into their past activities. Competitors may not necessarily be enemies."

"Sometimes they can be one and the same," James said but Jonathan had tuned him out.

Damion had asked Jonathan about enemies. Jonathan had said he wasn't aware of any, but his relationship with Johanna had conjured up memories of Sheryl he'd deliberately blocked from his mind.

Alex Colfax, the man Sheryl had really loved, had left Nottoway soon after her death. Glimpsing the coldness in the man's eyes at the graveside, Jonathan had wondered, for a fleeting moment, if the man grieved for Sheryl or if he was merely using her. He'd glimpsed more hatred toward Jonathan than grief from losing a loved one.

His last memory of Sheryl had been a nasty scene he'd never want repeated. Once he'd called the wedding off, she'd tried to reason with him.

"It was just a last fling before our lives would start together. I'll be a true wife to you. Honestly I will," she'd said.

Honestly. The fact that she'd used that word right after he'd caught her with Alex had him taking a second look at her and questioning his own judgment of character.

But Jonathan had glimpsed her face through the open curtains under the illumination of the living room lamp of his own cabin, and his heart had frozen as cold as an icy lake at what he'd seen that night. He'd never forget the scene.

She'd never gazed with such complete rapture and loving devotion when Jonathan had loved her. At that moment, he knew the words of devotion and love that had been spilling from her lips for the last year had been meaningless. They were just words she'd recited to get what she wanted. Not words of love ever after.

"No!" he'd said, "there won't be a wedding." He turned to leave the building, and heard a shout, seconds before a book hit him, bouncing off his shoulder.

When he focused on her, hatred gleamed from her eyes, not the love that had glowed less than five minutes before for another man.

"I never loved you. How could I when Alex owned my heart and soul?"

It was as if a strange woman had replaced the woman he thought he knew and trusted.

Jonathan approached the door, twisted the knob and looked back at her.

"I want you out of my cabin immediately. Leave the key on the table."

He opened the door and went out into the cold, dark March night. The night was fittingly as cold as the icicle that had lodged within him.

Automatically, he drove home, later unable to remember the trip at all. He only made it as far as the couch, his emotions anesthetized.

He'd still been there, in the same spot, when the call came two hours later, telling him that Sheryl had died instantly in a car crash.

Johanna had arrived shortly thereafter to comfort him. She'd stayed with him throughout the night. She'd been by his side, it seemed, every waking moment until Sheryl's body had been covered in her grave.

"Jonathan. Jonathan!" James touched his shoulder.

"What is it?" Jonathan asked, shaking off the memories.

"What is wrong with you? You were in a world of your own."

"Sorry, bad memories," he said.

"I'm going home. Are you okay?" he asked, skepticism lacing his voice.

"Yeah, spend some time with your family. You deserve it." Jonathan smiled to ease James' frown.

"I intend to do just that," James said slowly as he caught his jacket from the chair.

"Come on, man. Get out of here. You can't do anything else tonight. Let's see what Damion comes up with."

"Sure. I'll call Johanna. See if she's available tonight."

"For you? Anytime. If not, call Gladys. She'll make certain Johanna is," James chuckled and left.

"In the process I'd lose Johanna," Jonathan said into the silence of the office. He leaned back in his chair and watched his VP leave.

First, he needed to call Damion. Jonathan had an enemy Damion was unaware of. He trusted his chief of security to keep personal information confidential. He'd give only an abridged version of what had happened.

Some force drove him to Johanna's fresh spirit tonight. Seeing her was as crucial as water.

The light was still on in Johanna's cottage when Jonathan drove into her yard. He hadn't called her as he'd promised James. After talking to Damion, he'd left the complex and driven straight to her cabin.

He turned off the motor, opened the door and exited the Infiniti. He dug his hands into his pockets and walked to her door, trying to calm the demons that rode him. At her door, he inhaled fresh breaths to calm the adrenaline pumping through him and knew he'd failed.

Two quick raps against the door brought her there in seconds. He watched her standing there, looking gorgeous in her night clothing and happy to see him—just him.

The lamplight cast a glow on the white silk housecoat that delineated her curves. As she stepped back, he advanced through the door, shutting it behind him.

Her black hair fell across her shoulders, a sharp contrast to the white housecoat. Her medium-brown skin looked soft and sweet. She cocked an eyebrow, silently questioning his unusually somber mood.

"Hi." Her whisper-soft voice rushed over him, urging him to move.

He lifted his hands, stretched them into the folds of her wrap. Parting the lapels, he slid it off her shoulder. The fabric, as soft as her voice, floated from her arms to pool at her feet, exposing a matching short, spaghetti-strapped confection. Again the contrast of the gown against her skin was startling.

He touched her hands at her sides, sliding his fingers up her fingers, slowly past her hand and up her arms. When he reached her shoulders, he held her, and kissed her neck. He felt and heard her intake of breath. He lifted his head and clasped his lips to hers, gathered her warm body close to his. Then he parted her lips, mingled his tongue with hers, tasting the secrets of her hot, fresh mouth. Deepening the kiss, he tightened his arms around her and ground her pelvis against his hardness.

Her soft, exploring hands and soft, pliant body sent electric sparks soaring through him.

Breathing hard, he lifted his mouth from hers.

"Hi," he whispered in a hoarse voice.

"Wow!" she said, her hands clinging to his neck.

Watching her luminous eyes, he gathered her in his arms. In a few quick steps, he passed the living room and entered the darkened bedroom. Placing her in the center of the bed, he leaned on his elbow, pressing his lower body against hers.

Her moan had him kissing her again and touching her. Then, he sat up. When she cried out, he said. "I need light, I want to see you."

He reached for the lamp switch and flicked it on. He glanced at her face—her honest face—that expressed her desire for him.

He reached for the hem of her gown. Caressing her inner thigh, he slid the wispy fabric up. His mouth traveled the path of his fingers. Barely a scrap of silk covered her pelvis.

Under the pressure of her fingers on his shoulders, and the music of her sigh, he licked the line leading to her navel. Swirling a tongue around her navel, he leaned up to glimpse her face, a face that didn't lie.

Returning to her softness, he trailed a path to her breast, rubbing his face against the soft skin underneath.

Her knees imprisoned him as he leisurely circled the globe with his tongue. Reaching down, and sliding his palms into her panties, he grasped her hips with both hands, pressing her center tighter against him as he sucked on a rigid nipple.

Johanna cried out and rocked her hips against him. Her hands clawed at his sides, his back, his arms. Sliding his shirt upward, it bunched under his arms, exposing his dark skin. She clasped his head in her hand, leaned up and kissed him, her fingers swirling in his ear, and over his neck.

He touched her other breast and gazed at her face expressing her arousal as she closed her eyes, her need so great.

"Open your eyes," he demanded softly.

She opened them, telegraphing her need and, pulled his shirt over his head.

He needed her desire like life-giving oxygen.

He stood, unsnapped his jeans, shucked them along with his briefs. Bending, he pulled the prophylactic from his pocket, ripped open the packet and dropped it on her.

Taking the challenge, she picked it up and stroked him with her soft hands. He fell to his hands in his weakness. Touching his body, kissing his chest, she eased the protection on him.

He pressed his body against hers, pressing her into the mattress and spreading her thighs wide to accommodate him. Staring into her face, he entered her.

He stroked her, impaled her, basked in her sighs and groans, her fingers clutching his back, scoring his arms, her breasts pressed against his chest.

Her thighs tightened around his hips, her hips undulating against him. As passion mounted, he clasped her hips in his hands, sank deeper into her, harder in her, until she cried out, imprisoning him within her thighs and embrace. Jonathan lifted his head just long enough to glimpse her rapture, to feel her rapture as he exploded, crying out her name, his arms caging her soft body against his.

Johanna shifted her head to glance at Jonathan. Her head rested on his right shoulder, his left arm clasped underneath her breasts.

He'd turned the lamp to a soft glow before he'd tucked her close to him.

He looked at peace.

She was thankful she'd called Gerald Jarrod, her attorney, the minute she'd returned to the hotel. Otherwise, she wouldn't have been in the mood to appreciate this wild unbridled side of Jonathan.

After Gerald Jarrod had reassured her for twenty minutes, Johanna had finally calmed down.

What on earth had come over Jonathan? Standing in the door, not uttering a word, he reminded her of an Egyptian king—all powerful and male.

Johanna closed her eyes against the emotions that assaulted her. She'd never been loved like that, with a consuming, passionate need. Dow Jones averages and stock portfolios didn't begin to compare. Jonathan had locked that passionate side of himself away.

Some nagging suspicion made Johanna question what was going through his mind. He'd made love with a driving force, like the devil himself was riding him. But Johanna sensed the passion was there, that he'd wanted her—and only her.

Johanna wondered if he'd ever tell her what had been closest to his heart when he'd reached her door. Did he use her to drive away memories, or was this wave of passion because of his need for her?

She loved this passionate, untamed Jonathan and hoped to see more of him especially if his passion was a sign of growing affection.

CHAPTER 12

Sunday after early church services, Jonathan met Luke and Mrs. Drucilla at the Nottoway Country Club. They sat at an outside table, waiting for Johanna to show up. For the first time, he didn't recognize most of the people at the club.

One of the members snapped pictures for the bulletin board, a nice showpiece for advertising the success of the club, he'd said. Most of the visitors had purchased the golf package from the hotel.

"The club's doing well," he said to Luke as he glanced at his watch once again, wondering what could be keeping Johanna.

"Guests from the hotel are coming left and right," Luke said.

"Say, Jonathan," Luke continued, "the movie theater's really a hit. The investors had wondered if enough people live here to warrant a three-theater arrangement, but we've proven there are. Thanks for providing the extra money for the expansion and to keep the club going until we can get on our feet. I think the package deal with the hotel will bring us in the black."

"I can appreciate a good business deal as well as the next person," Jonathan said.

"Without you, the golf club wouldn't have lasted," Luke said.

"The average person who is as wealthy as you would want to own it. They wouldn't want to go in with a group like Luke's group," Mrs. Drucilla added.

"Our," Luke said correcting his wife. "You're a part of this, too, Drucilla. You signed the papers just like I did."

"I keep forgetting that. I'm part of the movers and shakers in Nottoway now. Isn't that something." She laughed at the very idea.

"That you are, Mrs. Drucilla. Luke's group planned this. I'm just one of many investors. You were part of shaping Nottoway even before the expansions." Jonathan replied.

"No. I was just an old woman trying to survive," Mrs. Drucilla said.

"The point is that you did survive, and well. Look at your children and grandchildren. Tylan's got three gas stations now. That entrepreneurial inclination started with you and your husband. You've got plenty to be proud of," Jonathan told her.

Luke put an arm around Mrs. Drucilla's shoulders as she uttered a nervous laugh. "But you, Jonathan, have put our little town on the map. You've made it possible for us to keep our youngens here instead of moving on to find work . . . . "

"Are you all ready? I'm ready to beat all of you." Tylan approached them with his pregnant wife, Clarice. She hadn't started to show yet.

All these pregnant women had Jonathan wondering

what it would be like to have a child of his own. His first thoughts of fatherhood began when Johanna moved back to town. He smiled at the thought of her pregnant with their child.

"Everybody's here except Johanna," Jonathan told him, looking in the direction of the parking lot.

"She'll be here soon. Someone detained her in the parking lot," Clarice said.

"Where is the little one today?" Jonathan asked.

"He's with his uncle Gerald and Theresa. They took him to the puppet show at the recreation center today. I have the funny feeling he's going to be pretty wired once he gets home," she said.

"He's wired all the time," Tylan lamented with fatherly fondness.

"Boys will be boys," Mrs. Drucilla said. "Tylan, you kept me running some as a youngen during the summers when you stayed with me. And you did, too, Jonathan. The mess the two of you could conjure up." She shook her head in memory. "You two kept me on my toes."

"I bet they did," Clarice said, her eyes dancing with delight at the fidgeting men. "But I'm sure you kept some healthy switches nearby to deal with them."

"Didn't have to use them much, though. They weren't bad boys, just a little mischievous."

"Talking about mischievous behavior, can you believe the nerve of that Samuel Smith?" Clarice asked. "He's got some nerve approaching Johanna about settling things between them. Like she'll willingly give a portion of her hotel to him."

"What are you talking about?" Jonathan asked, amusement forgotten.

"She didn't tell you?"

He shook his head. "No."

"That man approached her at the buffet last night—

the pig roast—and asked her to forget the lawyers and settle directly with him," Clarice continued. "Just hand over half of the business she worked, paid, and sacrificed for to him." The anger at the injustice simmered in her eyes.

"Hmm hmm," Mrs. Drucilla nodded her gray head. "That blabbermouth Darlene Thompson overheard them talking. Got some man to take her to the hotel, heard tell. She spread the news like a flood out of control," Mrs. Drucilla said. "Towanna told Luke about it last night. Phone woke me out of my sound sleep. Took me forever to get back."

Why didn't Johanna tell him? Jonathan wondered. True she wouldn't have had time when he first arrived, but she could have mentioned it later.

"Here she comes," Luke said and stood, helping Mrs. Drucilla to her feet.

Johanna rushed in, hair slightly windblown. "Sorry I'm late everyone. Have you been waiting long?"

"Just had a nice chat," Mrs. Drucilla said.

"Just in time for tee time," Luke said. "Well, it's time we started." He led the way out the door.

When the men stopped by the rental office for golf carts, the mayor and Tina approached them.

"Say, Luke," the mayor called out, "Tina and I couldn't get a tee time. You mind if we join you? I'd really like to talk to you and Jonathan about a business deal I've thought up. Got some ideas from the hotel guests last night."

Luke sighed and motioned to the other two couples. "You all go on. Drucilla and I will play with them. No sense in ruining everybody's day," he said under his breath.

Jonathan accepted the magnanimous gesture with grace. He wouldn't take Luke's place right now for anything. Eighteen holes of golf with those two would try the most dedicated saint.

As Jonathan, Johanna and the Chances walked away, he heard Mrs. Drucilla say, "I'll play golf with you, but you're not going to ruin my fun by talking business the whole eighteen holes. Make an appointment." She was about the only person in Nottoway who could get away with saying that and the mayor actually adhered to her wishes.

Jonathan's attention was riveted on Johanna. All windblown and slightly mussed, she looked enchanting. Laughter danced in her eyes, and the navy pants she wore with a yellow and green sweater lit up her face.

He linked his fingers with hers as they neared the golf carts. He'd golfed several times with the other couples, but he'd always felt like an outsider. They always invited him, wanting to include him in their lives and he hated to refuse their kind gesture.

Tylan and he had been best friends since they were children. For once, he didn't feel as though he were intruding on him and Clarice.

The special cohesion Jonathan felt wasn't just from being with any woman. It was Johanna and the way she illuminated his life.

Still, Jonathan's history with women taught him even the most loving ones could twist a man's life inside out. Though Karina and Phoenix repaired their relationship two years ago after their ten-year estrangement, he often wondered why Phoenix trusted her again. In the beginning, Jonathan believed the triplets were what brought them together again. But the couple seemed to really love each other. How could Phoenix forgive her after so many years? And didn't Mrs. Drucilla lead Luke a merry dance for decades. Yet now, with both of them hovering around eighty, they acted like teenagers fresh in love.

As Jonathan climbed into the cart and drove onto the course, he wondered if he could ever let his guard down enough to trust that kind of happiness again. He leaned and kissed Johanna lightly on the lips. Even as he carried his guard like a shield, she drew him like a magnet. After last night, letting her go would be tantamount to tearing part of his heart away.

After the game Johanna and Jonathan shared brunch with the two other couples at the Nottoway Inn.

"I'm so stuffed, I need to walk," Johanna said as they walked to the parking lot to retrieve Jonathan's car.

"We'll walk then."

"And leave your car here?"

"I need the exercise, I can get it later."

Jonathan clasped her hand in his and they strolled along the wide path where several guests milled about. The temperature had warmed and Johanna pulled off the sweater she wore and tied it around her waist.

The privacy gave him the perfect opportunity to discuss Samuel Smith.

"What's happening with Smith?" he asked her. "I heard about last night."

"Aside from his greed, just the sight of him gives me the creeps. Nothing has changed otherwise, except Mrs. Drucilla says his father was sterile from some childhood sickness."

"That's interesting."

"And Smith is still searching through family papers."

Jonathan made a mental note to have Damion do a thorough background check on Samuel Smith.

They reached the river. Boaters explored at a romantic, leisurely pace. Love was certainly in bloom on the delightful spring day. Farther down, he glimpsed fishing lines dangling into the water from several boats.

The wind blew and the faint aroma of Johanna's perfume—the same scent she'd worn last night drifted by him. His gut tightened. She looked fresh and inviting, walking beside him. He released her hand and drew his arm across her shoulders.

Jonathan found himself increasing their pace. If he didn't get his body under control, she'd soon think he was after only one thing from her, although all of her intrigued him. And now that she was within his grasp, he couldn't get his fill.

Even for propriety, Jonathan couldn't wait for her any longer. He needed to be a part of her as much as he needed water to survive and every bit as much as he'd needed her last night. When she'd become so crucial to him, he didn't know. He only knew that his desire for Johanna sneaked up on him suddenly.

Jonathan inserted the key in Johanna's door and opened it, letting her enter before him. Easing her back against him he let it click closed behind them. He had to have her again.

Wednesday after work, Jonathan changed clothes and hurriedly cleaned his house.

Tomorrow was cleaning day for Mrs. Perch, who was seventy-four and had been his housekeeper since Karina was fourteen. She refused to retire. Until he could convince her to do so, he couldn't hire anyone to replace her and he wouldn't force her out. The two times he'd broached the subject, she clucked her tongue about how much he needed her. And he had when Karina was younger.

At that time, she'd lived with them. But ten years ago, Jonathan had purchased an acre of land near her sister, who she liked to visit frequently, and built her a small home of her own with all the conveniences he could include without offending her. She'd been full of joy the day he'd presented it to her.

When Jonathan had offered to get her some help, she'd complained that he'd make more work for her by having to go behind the person to clean. *Youngens don't like to work like we did in my day.* So Jonathan made an attempt at cleaning each week before she arrived. Living alone, he didn't make much mess anyway.

He'd badgered her into getting extra help for window washing and the hard cleaning she liked done with the change of each season. The cleaning crew he let her select complained hard and long about her supervision, but Jonathan was left with a spotless house that shined suitably for a king.

When he first hired her, she was a hard worker and helped enormously with advice with Karina and encouragement whenever he needed it. The house was always spotless. As far as he was concerned, she'd earned a comfortable retirement.

He'd thrown the windows wide to catch the fresh air and had just sponged down the bath when he heard car wheels crunching on gravel in his drive. He'd left just enough work for her feel useful. She spent a full day in his house. And he was aware of the nap she took from eleven to one, which was fine by him.

Jonathan rinsed his hands and answered the door by the second knock.

"Making a stranger of yourself?" Tylan asked, crossing the threshold.

"No, cleaning."

Tylan laughed. "Mrs. Perch, hmm. Still feels she's got to take care of you."

"Something like that."

Tylan headed to the fridge, pausing to scan the contents. "What happened to the Becks?"

"Haven't had time to shop."

"Well, shucks." He pulled out a soda and shut the door. Unscrewing the cap, he took a long swallow. One would guess by his contented sigh that he'd been deprived.

"How did you get away from the little tyke?" Tylan's son was almost like his shadow. Jonathan didn't often see one without the other.

"I've got to pick him up from Grandma's. They're cooking. He wouldn't leave her until she made him corn pudding. That boy," Tylan lamented. "Got her wrapped around his finger, like Johanna's got somebody else wrapped around her finger." Tylan sat on the edge of the chair and rested his bare arms on his legs.

"Don't even go there," Jonathan told him. He marched to the fridge for his own soda.

Tylan set the drink on a coaster on the cocktail table and held up his hands. "I'm happy for you, man. You're due some happiness. Who'd have thought Johanna would turn out to be a looker. Those high waters she wore in high school embarrassed Mrs. Jones so badly. Remember when, in her junior year, she talked her mom into giving her the clothing budget to buy her own clothes? Convinced Gladys she was responsible enough to handle her own money."

Jonathan laughed, looking back on that episode with humor. "I remember."

"Smith had told her about some stocks and she decided she could wear the ones she had another year and invest the money."

"Gladys was fit to be tied."

"Showed up at the church picnic in August with her pants two inches too short."

"Gladys couldn't hustle her into the car and out of there fast enough."

"Umm hmm. She threatened to keep Johanna from that hotel. And look at her now. She couldn't have happened to a better guy." Tylan took another swallow of soda and grimaced. "Do you want to talk about it?"

Jonathan was silent for a moment. Then he said. "She's as different from Sheryl as night from day."

"How do you feel about that?"

"I just realized how much I enjoyed her company when she was underfoot with Karina. We could always talk. Of course I always thought of her as a little kid back then."

Tylan snorted. "Johanna was never a little kid. Even at six, she was a pint-sized adult."

"And then she moved back, all grown up," Jonathan said. "And I realized that . . . " He stood and ran a hand through his hair. "She threw me for a loop."

"Welcome to the club, buddy. I was getting tired of you being out here all by yourself." Tylan leaned back on the couch and put his hands behind his head.

"Come on out with it," Jonathan said to Tylan. He sensed another purpose for the visit. "Something's stirring in that head of yours."

"Did Sheryl's parents know what happened the night she died?"

"No . . . I don't think so. They never let on." Tylan was the only person who knew the truth about that night, because Jonathan trusted him.

"But are you sure they didn't know?"

Jonathan leaned forward. "Why? I never said anything to them. I never told them the wedding was off."

"But she might have been leaving her parents' house."

Jonathan backtracked fourteen years. "Well she died near there."

"Her parents said that she must have been going to your house."

"Tylan, let's leave it in the past."

"Was it because she told them what happened and they forced her to try to patch up the engagement?"

"Impossible. She knew I wouldn't marry her under any circumstances." Jonathan stood up and paced. "Above all, Sheryl wasn't a complete fool."

"Her parents doted on her. She was the shining apple of their eye. And Mr. Newton manages the filter department at Blake Industries."

"He's also a good, hardworking, honest man. Forget it." Jonathan refused to believe this good-natured man would put the livelihood of so many people in jeopardy.

"The question is, can you afford to forget it?"

"Ahh." Jonathan raked his hands through his hair again and bit off an expletive. "I'm going to prove you wrong."

"Please do," Tylan said. "As long as you still have a company."

Jonathan returned to the couch, dropped onto the cushion and scrubbed a hand over his face. They'd lost their only daughter. Even now he visited the Newtons, took Christmas and birthday presents. He

felt more sorrow for their loss then he ever did for
his own. They never saw the selfish streak in their
beautiful daughter. They could never see past her
beauty and their love. For a time, neither could he.

CHAPTER 13

Johanna broke the pencil she held in two at the news that twisted her insides into knots. Raymond Smith had one son by Sonya Davis. His name had been legally changed from Samuel Davis to Samuel Smith within months of his birth.

Her single ray of hope had been extinguished in one short phone conversation. She shuddered at the thought of sharing a business with that man. He was so unlike Smith. Perhaps he took after his mother's side of the family, Johanna thought.

She still hadn't pulled herself together when Jonathan arrived. While they stood in the doorway talking, Smith drove up in his blue pickup truck.

Travis peered out the passenger window and barked when he saw Johanna. Smith exited the truck, carrying a cardboard box. The dog dashed out behind him, and headed for Johanna, seeking affection. Johanna could use a bit herself.

"Hi, old boy," Johanna said, bending down, and ruffling his fur.

Travis gave Johanna a couple of happy barks.

"Fine day, isn't it?" Smith said to Johanna and Jonathan as he approached them.

"We're good, Smith. I'm going to have to fight your dog for my lady," Jonathan said. "Let me carry that box for you."

"He's a real ladies' man, all right," Smith chuckled, handing over the box.

Johanna rolled her eyes. "I'm surrounded by too many males. Let's sit out on the deck." She led the way with Travis. Curiosity got the better of her. "What's in the box, Smith?"

"I've found records on the different places Raymond lived. My father kept a file on where he mailed the checks. Uncle Raymond moved around every few years until he died. I don't know if that will help you, but I'll leave it."

"I'll take anything at this point." Then she relayed the news she'd just received.

"That's so unlike him not to tell us he had a child. We were estranged for most of his life but not in the end. He would have provided for a child, and as far as I know, he never married."

"One doesn't necessarily preclude the other," Johanna said.

"You know, he called my dad a few months before he died. He was really down in the dumps, and Dad was really worried about Uncle Raymond. Dad even talked him into coming home. He returned a month before he died." Smith scratched his chin. "I remembered it was like he just wasted away."

"Do you know what troubled him?"

"No. I didn't spend very much time with him. I was away part of the time."

"And your dad didn't say what happened?" she asked him.

"No, he didn't. Raymond just sat almost in a trance most of the time. Almost like he was grieving."

"He could have broken up with a lady friend." Jonathan reached for the box. "Do you mind if I take a look?"

Johanna shook her head.

Jonathan set the box on the table. Opening it, he flipped through old papers and canceled checks.

"Do you want to join us for dinner, Smith?"

"No. I'm dining with Luke and Mrs. Drucilla." He stood. "Guess I'll be on my way. Drucilla don't like for company to show up late." Without glancing at Travis, he said, "Time to go, Travis."

Travis jumped up from his resting place by Johanna's feet, and followed Smith down the steps.

"You know," Smith focused on his shoes, "if he really is my uncle's child, I don't mind sharing what I have with him. I don't need much. My houses are paid for. And you paid me a fair price for the hotel." He scratched his head and put his cap back on. "I didn't want all that money you paid me and I still don't." Then he scrubbed a hand along his stubbled chin. "Why hasn't he called me? I'm the only cousin he has?"

Johanna shook her head and smiled. "You've got such a generous heart."

Smith and Travis got in the truck and left.

Johanna stared out after them for a time, realizing that this was tough on Smith, as well.

"Do you mind if I take these things a day or two?" Jonathan asked, breaking the silence. "I'll see what I can come up with."

"Sure," Johanna said.

They went back to the deck, but Johanna wondered,

too, why Samuel Smith hadn't contacted his closest living relative on his father's side of the family.

On Friday night, Jonathan watched Johanna's derriere as she bent over to shove a pan onto the cabinet shelf. He wanted to snatch her and take her immediately to the bedroom. Worse, he wanted her every night.

Jonathan inhaled a deep breath. He went a little crazy every time he saw her, and he hadn't been his normal self since she arrived in Nottoway.

"Marry me, Johanna." Jonathan watched her as she straightened as if she'd received an electric shock.

"What!" She gulped several huge breaths.

"Will you?"

"I . . . " She grabbed a stool and sat. "Jonathan, I don't know what to say," she finally responded.

He leaned against the countertop and crossed his arms. "Yes, will be sufficient."

"But, I can't give a marriage the time it needs right now. I'm in the middle of planning a grand opening and I don't know what's going to happen with the hotel."

"Your insurance will cover that. I have problems to resolve, but I won't let it interfere with us. Regardless of the outcome, I'm financially stable and . . . " he moved toward her and stopped. Lifting a hand, he caressed her face and whispered. "I need you in my life, Johanna."

She closed her eyes, reaching up to touch his hand. "Oh, Jonathan," she sighed and opened her eyes. "I love you, too, but . . . "

"Marry me tomorrow," he entreated. "We can get the license today. We've got an hour to get to the courthouse."

When she remained silent, he said, "I've got a surprise for you."

Jonathan went to his car. In two minutes, he was back with a long, white garment bag.

"What?" Johanna's hands flew to her cheeks.

"It's a beautiful gown. I want to see you walk down the aisle to me in this dress."

"*You* picked out a gown for me?"

"With Paula's help. She knows your tastes." He handed the bag to her. "I hope you like it. I have the shoes to match—everything you need."

"We can't plan a wedding in one night. It isn't done," she said holding the bag up like a rag doll. "My family . . . " she continued inanely.

"We'll tell them tonight."

"Why the rush?"

He took the bag from her, placed it carefully across the sofa and gathered her in his arms. "What we have is very special. I don't want you to be the talk of the town in an unfavorable light." He lowered his voice, holding her against his warmth. "I want you beside me every night. When the triplets visit, I don't want you sneaking out in the middle of the night." He caressed her face. "We're perfect together," he whispered against her ear. "Can't you feel that special connection, too?"

Johanna felt it, all right. She never dreamed she'd love a man the way she loved Jonathan. "What about Sheryl? I won't be second best in your heart. When you marry me, I don't want your love for her to interfere in what we have together."

"Sheryl has been gone a very long time. I'm not the same man I was back then. It's you I want—you I need."

"Oh, Jonathan . . . "

"Say yes," he whispered, and just the texture of

his voice sent pure unabashed pleasure through her. How could she refuse him?

"Yes!" she whispered, and he pulled her tighter against him. Lowering his head, he kissed her—deep, demanding, a seal of their love forever.

"You're what!" Gladys' outraged bellow numbed Johanna's ears. She jerked the phone away from her ear, and shook her head before cautiously holding the receiver three inches away.

"Jonathan and I are getting married tomorrow," she repeated.

"Are you crazy? I can't plan a wedding in one day."

"Everything's already planned, Mom," Johanna explained patiently. "You don't have to do anything but show up."

"You always did do things the crazy way. We can't book the church, get the preacher, plan the wedding party, get the gowns made, plan the dinner all in one day, Johanna! It's six o'clock for goodness' sake. Do you hate me that much?" Halfway through the tirade, Johanna counted to ten. Jonathan took the phone from her.

"Hello, Mrs. Jones." His tone was affable. "Johanna and I thought a nice intimate wedding with the family would be more appropriate. We've got the church booked at one. Will that be a problem for you?"

"Oh, Jonathan," Gladys said with an immediate change in tone. "If that's what you want, we'll all be there. Are you sure you don't want a big wedding? You know, to invite your friends and business associates."

Jonathan never had problems with the moms. Gladys Jones was no exception.

"Actually, we'll plan a large reception later when

Johanna and I aren't so busy. With so much on our plates, we can't take the time out right now."

"I have plenty of time on my hands. I don't mind doing it."

"Johanna will be happy to get your help on the reception. I know you'll do a wonderful job as you do in everything you do."

"That's the least my future son-in-law can expect," Gladys informed him. "Well, I guess I better come over and help Johanna get things straight for tomorrow."

"It's all taken care of, Mrs. Jones. All you need to do is show up at the wedding. Johanna and I plan a quiet evening in."

"Oh, well. In that case, I'll see you tomorrow."

"I'm looking forward to it. Johanna has made me the happiest man in the world."

Henry Jones, urged by his wife's prodding, came by within the hour to give Jonathan that father-in-law-to-prospective-groom talk. Ending with, "If there is ever a time where you can't treat Johanna with the kindness and respect she deserves, send her back home."

It was a good thing Gladys wasn't there. She'd have singed Henry's ears for a year if she'd heard those words. Her most troublesome offspring was to marry Jonathan at all costs. Plenty of time later to discuss the rest.

After Henry left, Johanna and Jonathan snuggled on the couch to watch *Stormy Weather*. Johanna was in an old movie mood tonight.

"What are you thinking about?" Jonathan asked her, stroking her arm with a light touch.

She glanced at him and sighed. "About this sudden decision of yours."

His arm tightened around her. "Do you want to marry me, Johanna?"

She gazed directly at him. "Yes," she whispered, touching his beloved face.

"Then that settles it."

"These sudden decisions aren't like you." But Johanna knew she was lost once he gave her that sweet, crooked smile.

"You don't think I can be spontaneous?"

"I didn't say that. It's just . . . marriage is a big step."

"Don't think I don't know that. If I wasn't sure of my feelings for you, I wouldn't marry you, Johanna."

He lowered his head and kissed her upturned face, marking a path of soft kisses to her lips. By the time his lips touched hers, Johanna had forgotten about any reservations she had about marriage with Jonathan. Forgotten was Sheryl and how much he'd loved her. Johanna was in his life now. And that was what she'd reflect on.

After Jonathan released her, he dug into his pocket and pulled out a jeweler's box. "I know women like to choose their own rings. You can choose your own once we're married, but I hope this will do temporarily."

He opened the box to a sparkling five-carat diamond. Johanna sucked in a breath and held. "I'll be afraid to wear anything this lavish."

"This is nothing in comparison to the joy you give me, sweetheart."

A sudden dampness sprang to her eyes. "I don't have anything for you."

"I took the liberty in choosing a set for us. Again, you can change it later." He pulled out another box with matching platinum wedding bands for both of them.

Ahh, Jonathan. Can I afford to pay you for your ring?"

"I don't expect you to pay me." He tapped her on the nose with a playful stroke.

"That's one concession I won't make. I will pay you. A groom shouldn't have to pay for his own ring."

"We'll talk about that later." He eased her into another kiss.

"As tempting as your kisses are," she said as she wrapped her hand around his neck and touched his cheek with the back of her fingers, "I won't forget. I'm adamant about that, Jonathan."

"All right. Anything to please my bride-to-be," he whispered against her lips.

Tomorrow this time, she'd be a bride. Johanna splayed her fingers against the back of his head, feeling the soft hair against her fingers, and urged him toward her.

An urgent knock rattled the door. Sliding out of his arms, Johanna padded across the carpet and opened it to a frantic Pamela.

"What do you want me to wear tomorrow?" she asked, barging in to the room. She glanced around the cabin. "What are you doing relaxing? We have to go shopping. I don't have a thing to wear!" She paced about using harried steps. "What's Jonathan doing here? Aren't you supposed to be doing some guy thing the night before your wedding?"

"Nope." Jonathan stood with an easy, fluid grace. "Johanna and I are spending a quiet evening together."

Pamela ran over and pulled him toward the door. "Hit the door, buster. We've got too much to do for you to be hanging around."

"But . . ." Jonathan stopped in his tracks and refused to budge.

"Pam. What is wrong with you? It's going to be a small, intimate wedding. Only family will be there."

"You don't need to buy anything," Jonathan said.

"I'm your matron of honor. You're marrying the most prominent man in the town and I don't have anything to wear. That's what's wrong! We're going to pick Mom up and shop at Paula's. She's staying open just for us and she has a seamstress nearby to make alterations if we need to."

"This is silly. You have a closet full of semiformal wear." Johanna wondered if some of her mom's hysterical tendencies had rubbed off on her sister.

Pam ignored Johanna.

Another knock pounded on the door. Jonathan raked a hand over his head and sucked in a breath. Then he opened it.

It was Gladys Jones.

"Jonathan, you may as well go home. We've got to at least get some flowers in the church by tomorrow. She can't walk down the bare aisle. I've gotten five calls in the last hour. It's all over town that you got a wedding license today."

"I've already seen to the flowers, Mrs. Jones."

"What color scheme did you use? I hope you didn't choose some awful color."

"Johanna's favorite. Green."

"Green," Mrs. Jones said. "Have you ever seen a wedding with green flowers?"

"The bows and what-nots are green. I left it up to the florist to choose the color of the flowers. I trust her tastes."

"You . . ."

"Which florist? We've got to give her a call."

"Mom, calm down. There's only one florist in Nottoway, but you're making me nervous. It's just a simple family wedding.'' Johanna felt like a tape recorder.

"With Jonathan, nothing's simple. You'd do well to remember that, young lady." Then she rounded on her other daughter. "Pam, we've got to pick out a green gown for you. She turned around and glanced at Jonathan. "Goodnight Jonathan."

Jonathan put an arm around Mrs. Jones' shoulders, another around Pam's and eased them to the door. "Why don't you ladies shop to your heart's content. Johanna and I will stay here."

The tactic didn't work.

"It's Johanna's wedding. You shouldn't be with her tonight, anyway."

Jonathan should have known better than to try to reason with a determined group of women. A man just couldn't win.

He had just enough time to give Johanna a quick kiss before Gladys hustled him out the door, shutting it in his back.

He wished they'd eloped.

As soon as the door shut, Gladys rounded on Johanna. "You've finally got the richest man in town to marry you and what do you do? You sneak off for a tiny wedding instead of waiting to put on a grand affair. You could have had the wedding of the century."

"We should have eloped," Johanna told her mom.

"Hush your mouth!" Gladys admonished.

Resigned, Jonathan wondered why he hadn't asked Johanna to wait until tomorrow to call her family. As he backed up his car to turn it around, he heard a wild screech erupt from the cabin and wondered what Johanna had done this time to aggravate Gladys. Putting the car in drive, he accelerated and drove away from the last of his anticipated quiet wedding eve with Johanna. He'd drag Tylan from whatever he was doing. He was the best man, after all. Jonathan wasn't in the mood to spend the night alone.

Johanna stood apprehensively at the church door with her father. Instead of the relaxing evening she and Jonathan had planned, she'd had a taxing few hours shopping with her mother.

Even though the wedding was informal, Jonathan had arranged escorts for seating, which was a good thing because it took the starch out of Gladys' shoulders. A photographer had even arrived at Pam's house where Johanna dressed before James drove her parents and her to the church.

"The church is almost full. Word travels," Pam whispered to Johanna after peeping through the vestibule door.

"Your mom spent half the night on the phone," Henry said.

"Oh, no," Johanna moaned.

"You know Gladys." Her dad patted her hand. "Don't you worry about it. There's nothing you can do anyway," he sighed a long-suffering sigh. "I learned a long time ago," bemoaned a man who had lost many arguments with his determined wife.

A whispered, "They're ready," came through the door.

Pam struck a pose and started down the aisle.

"You do love Jonathan?" her dad asked as her sister floated farther and farther away.

"Yes, I do."

He hugged her, then tried to straighten her veil. "Be happy, daughter. You were a strong-minded child and grew up to be an equally strong woman. Never accept anything less than the best. That's one of the qualities I've admired about you. And remember, you'll always have a home."

"Thank you, Dad." She stood on tiptoe and kissed his weathered cheek. It seemed like only yesterday when, almost on a daily basis, her mom had sent Johanna to him for a scolding. His calm, reassuring voice had always been soothing. It still had the power to calm her jangled nerves.

Remembering her mother strutting down the aisle brought a smile to Johanna. At least she'd finally done something Gladys was proud of.

Karina must have stayed up most of the night to plan the lavish wedding banquet the guests and wedding party attended. Even Tylan and Pam had a prepared toast.

They even received a few gifts from people who had hurried out to shop first thing that morning.

Johanna's chef had arrived with a crew carrying the sliced and chopped barbecue Johanna was so fond of, a huge cake he bemoaned that he'd stayed up all night preparing, and lavish desserts.

"Never let it be said that the Nottoway Inn can't rise to the occasion," Albert whispered with due *hauteur*.

By the time Jonathan left the reception with Johanna who was still dressed in her long, white gown, Gladys Jones was beaming. He'd have to add extra in the check to Karina for ordering extra food for the dinner. Turned out, the church had filled by the time the wedding was over. And instead of the small, intimate, cozy affair he'd planned, it turned into a large gathering. Who else could have assembled a church load of people on the loveliest Saturday in May—where the temperature hovered around seventy degrees, with no rain in sight when the last two Saturdays rain had poured—in merely one night? And she still had time to buy a new dress and shoes, drag the hairdresser out of bed at 5:00 A.M., and drive Karina and her staff crazy along with Johanna's restaurant employees. At 1:00 A.M., Jonathan was still getting calls of confirmation. Gladys Jones was an amazing woman.

What the wedding lacked in preparation, it made up for in the food and atmosphere.

He glanced at Johanna who looked like a milk chocolate confection dressed in white lace.

"Where are we going?" she asked.

"On a short honeymoon. Every bride deserves one."

"And groom. How short?" she asked referring to the honeymoon.

"Early Monday morning I'll deliver you to your office."

They were driving north on Interstate 95 with just a smattering of traffic.

In another forty-five minutes they drove into Richmond and Jonathan pulled up into the Marriott's yard.

"You're supporting the competition, you traitor."

Jonathan leaned over and linked his fingers behind her head. "The Marriott's not competition for you. Besides, if we stayed at your hotel, you'd be tempted to work instead of concentrating on your new husband."

Johanna leaned toward him and kissed him. "Definitely not." Her kiss hastened his departure from the car.

Jonathan opened his door and rounded the hood

to assist. Gathering the yards of fabric, lace and veil, they made their way through the lavishly appointed lobby to the executive desk for a speedy check-in. Observing the staff, the decor and surroundings, she assured herself that the Nottoway Inn was indeed a classy hotel in every right. In moments, a bellman escorted them to their suite. This was the beginning of their lives together.

Johanna had married her dream man.

Mrs. Perch had hired a crew over the weekend to get the house spitting-clean for Jonathan's new bride. However, the afternoon after they returned from their short honeymoon, she promptly retired, stating that, now that Jonathan had a wife to take care of him, she could retire with peace of mind.

Since moving to Nottoway, Johanna's cabin had been cleaned daily along with the other hotel rooms and cabins. She didn't look forward to sponging bath-rooms and mopping floors after fifteen-hour work-days. What time would she have left for Jonathan now that she only had a month before the grand opening?

She hoped Jonathan kept a neat house. Then she realized there was so much she really didn't know about him.

CHAPTER 14

By Tuesday night, all of Johanna's clothing shared closet space with Jonathan's. He'd cleaned out several drawers for her. Her books joined his on the bookshelves located in the den and great room.

The cabin she'd used had been readied for rental to paying customers. The desk, chairs and bookshelves in the second bedroom had been replaced by twin beds and a dresser. A sudden peace descended on Jonathan now that Johanna had settled under his roof. Forcibly, he concentrated on the meeting.

"We've weeded out the distributor and the trucker," Damion said Thursday afternoon in a meeting with James and Jonathan. "Which means the switch occurred here. I personally checked several batches and found bad filters stored among the good ones. Not many, but they were there."

"That's progress, now that the search has narrowed," Jonathan said.

Sheryl's father. Once Tylan had planted the seed in Jonathan's mind, it had been impossible to dislodge the thought. Yet, he couldn't fathom that the quiet, dedicated man could be responsible for Blake Industries' troubles.

"Make sure every filter is checked before it leaves the grounds," he said to James.

Then he turned to his chief of security, "Have you looked at the records of all the employees in that department, especially the new ones?"

"We're still going through them. And we've stepped up security all over."

"If that's all, Jonathan," James interrupted, "I have another meeting in five minutes."

"That's it," Jonathan told him.

After the door closed behind James, Jonathan had one last question he dreaded. He'd prefer to think Alex Colfax was responsible than to consider Ronald Newton.

"Have you found anything on Alex Colfax?"

"His last known address is in New Mexico. That was two years ago. There's nothing since."

"And Samuel Smith?"

"There was definitely a child who was born in Alabama. Raymond Smith is named as the father on the birth certificate. Samuel Smith attended school there until the fifth grade. The family moved after that. They moved constantly. The ten-year stretch in Alabama was the longest in one location, it seemed. We're continuing to check each location, but the man didn't apply for a Social Security number until ten years ago. It's as if he disappeared from age ten to thirty-five. Last, Raymond Smith never married."

Damion was a man of few words, so Jonathan asked him. "How can someone function without a Social Security number? What's your suspicion?"

"Social Security numbers popping up at odd times sometimes means a stolen identity. After all, a Social Security number is required for employment. Where did he work before he reached thirty-five without one?"

"Perhaps he didn't have a legitimate job. Johanna says he reminds her of . . . an unsavory character," he amended his wife's description.

"Raymond Smith traveled a great deal. We have more states to check." He stood, signaling that he had no more information to impart. "I'll get back to you soon," he said and left.

Friday afternoon at six, Johanna was so exhausted she felt she could sleep for a week, but she remained at her desk to finish more paperwork before leaving for home. Before she could get away, her mother stopped by.

"Why are you still at work with a new husband at home?" Gladys glanced around the office before making her way to a chair. She wore a beige jogging suit with burgundy decorative stitching.

Johanna glanced at her watch. "I didn't realize it was so late," she said. "It's good to see you, Mom."

"I just left your house. Your poor husband hadn't eaten dinner yet."

"I'll take something home from the hotel dining room then."

"A man likes some homemade food cooked by his wife now and then. He gets tired of hotel food and takeout. He settled for that when he was single."

"I fixed dinner yesterday, Mom. It may not be the greatest, but it didn't kill him, either. It's his turn today. We take turns preparing dinner."

"His turn?"

"Yes, he can cook better than I can, and we both work. We share the tasks."

"Men like for their women to cook."

"He wouldn't have married me then. I'm not a fantastic cook and you know it." Will there ever be an end to the nagging, Johanna wondered?

"Now that you're married, it's time you learned. I'll be happy to teach you," she offered.

"Mom, there's more to a marriage than cooking. Besides I don't have time for cooking lessons right now, but thanks."

"It's a woman's job to see that her husband is well fed. I've always had a nice hot dinner prepared for your father. I never neglected my wifely duties," her mom continued.

Johanna entwined her fingers very tightly together on her desk, and managed a tight smile. "You never worked a full-time job outside the home, either, Mom. I do."

"Did you resent that fact when you were growing up, Johanna?" Gladys snapped.

"Of course not. I don't have a problem with the way you lived your life. I just prefer to live my life differently, that's all. I wasn't criticizing you."

"Well, work or not, men haven't changed. The way to his heart is still through his stomach and his breeches. You'd do well to listen to what I'm telling you."

"Tonight, he'll settle for hotel food. Albert's a wonderful cook. There's nothing wrong with him preparing a dinner now and then."

Her mom ignored that statement. "Karina is a wonderful cook, too. He didn't marry you to cook for you, but that's what I caught him doing. Cooking and cleaning for goodness' sake. If he's going to do the housework why does he need you?"

"Oh, that's so nice of him. Perhaps because he loves me."

"You're missing the point, Johanna. Now that you've got him, you've got to make sure you keep him. Sheryl was a homebody. Just remember that's what he likes. A nice clean house and a filled belly. You aren't doing either right now."

"He's not married to Sheryl, Mom. He's married to me. I know how to handle my home."

"Let's just make sure he stays married to you. You need to leave work in enough time in the evenings to take care of home."

A nagging headache started in Johanna's temple. "You've given me the perfect solution, I'll hire a housekeeper. I'll talk to my housekeeping manager Monday morning. She'll have some suggestions."

"And why can't you do it?"

"Because I'm working twelve- and fourteen-hour days, that's why! I clean a little but it wouldn't hurt to have someone come by once a week to give the house a thorough cleaning." Johanna made a notation on her calendar.

"Don't you mess around, smarty pants, and lose that man. You hear me?"

Johanna sighed, at the end of her patience. "Mom, you're driving me crazy again. I take care of my husband in my own way."

They sat glaring at each other for moments.

"Come by the house for Sunday dinner," Gladys ordered.

Johanna sighed again, still peeved.

"You won't have to cook," Gladys assured her. "Pam, her family and Emmanuel are coming. Give us a chance to welcome Jonathan to the family."

"I'll see if Jonathan is free," Johanna said rubbing

her forehead. "Would you like me to bring a dish—if we come?"

"No, I'll take care of it since you're so busy." She rose from her seat. "Well, it's time for me to get home."

"I'll walk you to your car."

Gladys let out a long-suffering sigh. "You've always done your level best to ignore my advice," she berated her middle offspring as she clutched her purse in her hand.

Johanna had heard that statement a million times. She closed and locked the office door. Her secretary had left for the weekend. "That's not true," she answered for the millionth time.

"Well I'm finally glad you've taken my advice about something. Marrying Jonathan has truly pleased me."

"Mom, if I didn't love Jonathan, I wouldn't have married him. I'm sure you wouldn't want me to marry someone who I'd be miserable with just to please you." Her mother hadn't crossed her mind when Jonathan popped the question.

Gladys declined an answer as they exited the lobby.

Johanna had been married one week and already she was an inadequate wife in her mother's mind. But then, she never did anything right according to Gladys—except marry Jonathan.

Johanna left after seeing her mother off. Her gas gauge was near empty. She drove by Tylan's, filled her tank and waited in the usual Friday evening line to pay.

Tylan had three lines going, as usual, with the extra traffic that occurred on Fridays. In the line next to Johanna's was Mrs. Newton.

"Johanna," she said, "congratulations on your marriage."

"Thank you, Mrs. Newton."

"If I'd been invited, my husband and I would have attended."

"It was a rushed affair planned the evening before the wedding. The original plan was to have a reception later on."

"I see. Well I'm so happy Jonathan's finally found someone to care for him. I thought he'd never get over Sheryl. Their relationship was so special, you know?"

"Yes," Johanna said and wondered how people could be so callous.

"I remembered Sheryl often talked of you playing with little Karina as children. My, my, time does pass, doesn't it?" She sighed and shook her head.

"Yes, it does." People wouldn't let Johanna forget that Sheryl was there first. But Johanna tried to still her unsettling thoughts. Sheryl had been the Newtons' only child, after all. Johanna's heart went out to Mrs. Newton for her loss. "Do you still grow roses?" Johanna asked her. At one time, the Newtons' garden had been a showplace.

"No," she said shaking her head, a sadness stealing over her features. "I just haven't had the energy for them in years."

"That's sad. They were truly beautiful," Johanna told her. "I enjoyed driving by just to look at them."

Mrs. Newton merely smiled a vacant smile, but she didn't comment.

It was finally Johanna's turn at the register. "It was good seeing you," Johanna told the older woman.

"Take care of yourself, you hear?"

Between the confrontation with her mother and the brief dialogue with Mrs. Newton, Johanna was on edge by the time she reached home, but seeing Jonathan's welcoming face as he lit candles around the room, lifted her spirits immeasurably.

The aroma emerging from the kitchen reminded her of how hungry she was.

"What's the occasion?" Johanna asked him as she shoved her briefcase into the closet.

"We were engaged exactly one week from tonight. And we didn't get to view our old movies." With a dish towel in hand, he approached her and encircled her in his arms and nuzzled her neck. "I thought we could make up for it tonight."

"Ummm. You are a romantic. I like that." Johanna clasped her hands behind his neck and kissed him, and snuggled close.

"We have a half hour before dinner," he whispered in her ear.

Johanna inhaled his fresh, clean scent and knew she needed to clean up. "I'm going to take a quick shower, okay?"

"Dinner will be ready when you're through." He kissed her again before she slid out of his arms and made for the bedroom.

He followed her. "Johanna, Friday night, two weeks from now, I have to attend a special dinner with the mayor."

"Oh, how horrible."

"Warren's not that bad."

"I'll reserve judgment." She stepped out of her skirt and hung it, with the jacket, on the door.

Jonathan sat on the bed and watched her. "I want you there with me."

Johanna glanced at him. "You want to share your misery." She slid her hose down her legs.

"Whatever. It's important that you're there. Think you can make it?"

She padded over to him and bent to paste a quick kiss on his lips. "For you? Of course I can."

"Mark it on your calendar. It's a black tie-affair. You might want to visit Paula's for something special." Grabbing her about the waist, he toppled her onto the bed.

"Is anything special going on?" Her hand stroked his chest.

His voice was thick. "I want my new wife with me."

"I'll wear something nice."

He lowered his head. "Ummm. You look nice now."

"Jonathan, I need . . . "

"Later," he said and finished the job she'd started.

On Tuesday, Damion visited Jonathan's office at twelve, just as he was about to leave for lunch.

"I've got some news," Damion told him.

"What is it?" Jonathan asked.

He handed a large manila envelope to Jonathan. "Samuel Smith died when he was eleven in a car accident with his mother."

"So Raymond Smith did have a child. And that explains why the man posing as Samuel never visited his uncle. Do you know who he is?" Jonathan asked him.

"No. Do you want me to continue searching?"

Jonathan shook his head. "We'll let her lawyer handle it from here. We've done our part."

"All the information is documented inside."

"Thank you," Jonathan told the man as he walked out the door. Damion may not be much for small talk, but he got the job done. Jonathan liked that about him.

So, Johanna's intuition was correct. She'd be pleased that she didn't have to do business with "Samuel Smith" after all. Sad for Smith though. The older man was looking forward to getting to know his cousin.

Smith took the news in stride, even though he was upset that he wouldn't be getting to know a cousin.

"I know your heart was set on meeting this cousin," Johanna said to Smith as he stored his suitcase in the pickup bed. The day after the announcement, he'd packed his one bag for departure as quickly as the first time.

"That's the way it goes sometimes," Smith said and opened the door for Travis. He handed the house key to Johanna.

Johanna pocketed it and gave the dog one last pat before he leaped into the truck, and settled his rump in the passenger's seat.

"I'll store your papers back in the house."

"No rush. I won't be needing them any time soon."

"Smith. You do have a family, you know. You've always been part of my life. You'll always be loved." She reached up and hugged him.

He hopped from foot to foot after, clearly uncomfortable with the affection. "Shucks, I know that, gal." He looked toward the sky, weary of any sentimental offering. "Looks like good traveling weather. No clouds in sight."

"According to the weatherman anyway."

"I'll be back for the opening. Be staying the summer. Can't take that Florida heat."

"Good." The grand opening was a little more than two weeks away.

"I'll put on a suit, but I'm not wearing a tux," he warned Johanna.

"I don't expect you to," Johanna said as she eyed the freshly washed chambray shirt and fishing vest that he wore. The casual clothing suited him just fine.

CHAPTER 15

Where the dickens was Johanna? Jonathan glanced at his watch for what must have been the hundredth time. He'd called the hotel earlier and left a message with her secretary to remind her of tonight, but she hadn't been in at the time and the secretary didn't know when she'd return. *So, where the devil was she?*

The chair next to him on the stage that had been reserved for her was noticeably vacant during dinner. Jonathan forced the tasteless food down. He felt the emptiness inside him as anger sliced deeper into his gut. In the three weeks of their marriage, he'd asked only one thing of her. To be present for the mayor's dinner.

He was aware that the man irritated her to no end. Warren had the tendency to irritate Jonathan, too. But when you moved in the business world, entertaining people you'd rather not was one of the inconveniences you just had to put up with. She should understand.

The surprise of the evening was that the governor had attended the function.

An hour later, he honored Jonathan for his help in providing jobs and social amenities to the town and helping to steer Nottoway toward becoming the town with the lowest unemployment rate in the country, which also contributed to the lowest crime rate. Mixed emotions flowed through Jonathan. He'd accomplished his goals. If only he could solve his company's problems, all would be well.

When he stood to accept the plaque, Jonathan saw his sister and her husband. He saw Gladys Jones smiling encouragement toward him and her husband, Henry. He saw Pam and James, but when he glanced at his own table, he still saw an empty chasm where his wife should have been. He'd looked forward to seeing his wife on the stage with him.

Johanna was so fatigued she could scream when she fit the key into the lock at eleven-thirty that night and entered the great room. It was as quiet and still as if she were the only occupant. She headed straight for the couch and plunked into the cushions, not bothering to turn on the lights. Leaning her head against the back cushion, she closed her eyes. She just needed a short rest before she'd shower for bed. Jonathan would be fast asleep by now.

"Where were you?" Jonathan's voice from nearby startled her. The cold tone he used cut into her peace and immediately put her back up.

"At work. Where else?" she snapped. Her eyes remained closed.

"Right. Where else?"

Johanna lifted her head and pried open her gritty eyes to peek at him.

He stood across the room with his back toward her, gazing out the window.

For the first time, Johanna really stared at her husband. "Look, I've had a very long week." She rubbed her neck. "I'm not up to any sarcasm tonight," she snapped but the words held only a little starch.

"You're not up for very much lately, are you?" She heard the ice click against the glass and saw his arms move to carry the drink to his mouth.

"I'm not arguing with you tonight. I'm going to bed." Johanna stood and left the room. Once she entered the bedroom, she peeled off her clothes and headed to the shower, wondering at his strange mood.

No long, leisurely shower tonight, she thought, as the hot water pounded her drained body. She didn't have an ounce of energy left.

Afterwards, she quickly toweled off and applied lotion in her favorite scent. A certain unsettling sensation mixed with the fatigue, making it impossible for her to relax. What was with Jonathan? Pulling on an old T-shirt she padded into the bedroom in her bare feet, and stopped short when she saw him.

Slowly, he unbuttoned the last button on the shirt he wore with his tux.

Then she remembered. He'd asked her to attend a dinner with him tonight. The mayor was in attendance.

"Oh, Jonathan. I'm so sorry," she stepped closer to him. "I completely forgot about Warren's dinner."

Jonathan didn't even look at her as he shrugged the white shirt off his wide shoulders. "It's okay." Dropping the shirt on the bed, he sat on the edge and pulled off his dress shoes and socks with jerky movements.

As fatigued as she was, he still looked good to her and she had to mentally stop herself from charging to him and running her hands across his shoulders. But she'd disappointed him.

"It's not okay," she said, taking another step toward him. "I had to run to Richmond and . . ." She crossed her arms under her breasts. "This opening has me going so . . ." she stopped.

"The rest of your family was there." He neglected to look at her.

It wasn't the same he'd left unsaid. She was his wife. She should have been there, too. "It was a dinner. What was the big deal?" she asked him.

He glanced at her then, the barely checked anger startling her. "The big deal was that I asked you to come. Couldn't you even pencil me on the calendar?"

"Jonathan, you're being unreasonable. Okay, so I forgot to pencil it in that night. We spent such a magnificent evening together, and later I just didn't think of it again."

"Would you have forgotten a meeting, Johanna? After all, that's important to you."

"What is wrong with you? You know you're important to me. The two don't compare." She rubbed a hand up and down her arm. "It was a dinner for heaven's sake."

He stood, unzipped his trousers with jerky motions, let them drop, and stepped out of them. He pulled on a pair of old jeans and slid them over his hips. "Yeah," he nodded, "it was just a dinner with *your husband.*"

When the phone rang, he ignored it, and Johanna strode to the bedside table and picked it up. It was her mother.

"Johanna?"

Johanna couldn't take her mother's badgering tonight.

"Not now, Mom. I'll call you tomorrow. Good-bye." She hung up the phone, faced Jonathan and tried to reason with her husband again.

"It *was* just a dinner, wasn't it, Jonathan?" she asked cautiously.

"Don't worry about it, Johanna." He stalked out of the bedroom and out the back door.

Well, if he was going to be unreasonable about it. Johanna stomped to the bed, picked up his shirt, and sat on the edge, at a loss as to what to do or say. She couldn't leave the atmosphere strained between them.

She held the shirt next to her face and inhaled his scent, a combination of soap, a splattering of spicy cologne and his own male essence.

She rose, tossed it into the hamper and marched into the great room, turning on the light. She could use a glass of water. And then she'd join her husband outside. She started for the kitchen when a reflection from the table caught her eye. Padding over there, she saw a plaque and picked it up. It was from the governor's office.

It was a special commendation.

She exhaled audibly through her lips. No wonder her family had been there. Why didn't he tell her he was receiving a special award? *Why hadn't he called her earlier today?*

Slowly, she went to the patio door and opened it. Closing it behind her, she neared her husband, reached out and touched his back. His muscles stiffened under her fingers.

"Jonathan, talk to me."

"I asked one thing, only one thing of you, Johanna, and you couldn't even do it."

"I didn't know. You should have told me. You know how busy I am."

"I'm busy, too, but I take *some* time out for you. It's got to go both ways, you know."

"I understand that. It will be better after the opening in a week."

"Are you sure about that? I know how focused you can be. It's probably my fault for rushing you into something you weren't ready for."

"You knew I worked when you married me. I'm not a homebody like Sheryl. You knew that."

"What does Sheryl have to do with this?" he snapped out in frustration. "Everything with you goes back to Sheryl. Well, Sheryl wasn't missing tonight. You were!"

"I didn't say she was." Heaven forbid she say something about his precious Sheryl.

"She didn't love me. But she certainly showed up at social obligations, if nothing else."

Sheryl may not have loved him, but he'd loved her.

"I don't like the comparisons, Jonathan."

"You're the one who brought her up, who's *always* bringing her up. Not me," he roared, slicing the air with his hand and leaning on the rail.

She strove for calm. "How did it go tonight?" she asked quietly.

"Why do you care?"

"I care. Don't close me out. I know apologizing is inadequate. It's just . . . "

"It wasn't important enough. *I* wasn't important enough. Is that it?"

"That's not true and you know it."

"Do I Johanna? Can you love anything as much as you love that hotel?"

"Why do women have to understand when men work overtime, but the situation isn't reciprocal."

"It is reciprocal. I understand. I cook the food, I clean the house. All I asked was for you to appear at one function in three weeks of marriage. Just one function. Was that too much to ask?"

Johanna sighed. "No."

"Who are you married to, Johanna, the hotel or me?" He didn't give her a chance to answer before he barked, "Go to bed, Johanna."

"I missed your awards dinner and I've apologized. Can't you let it go?"

He swiped a hand across his face. "Yes, I can let it go. Now, go to bed."

They silently listened while the crickets and frogs serenaded them. "Aren't you coming to bed with me?"

"I've got to finish packing for the trip. I'm leaving for Singapore tomorrow."

"Why didn't you tell me you were leaving?"

Seconds ticked by before he slid one glance in her direction. "I did, Johanna."

She walked to the edge of the deck with labored steps. She couldn't remember him telling her. "It really will get better after the opening. Just bear with me until then, okay?"

"Sure," he finally said, too quickly, much too quickly. He lifted the glass to his lips and swallowed.

"Can I help you pack?"

"No. Just go to bed. Let me finish my drink in peace. Please."

"I hope you aren't going to sulk."

He didn't dignify that with an answer.

It was a moment before she turned and trod to the house. Opening the patio door, she made her way slowly back to the bedroom. Once there, she sat on the side of the bed and reflected on her husband's disappointment and her mother's nagging words.

Perhaps she'd been so focused on her beloved hotel that she neglected her husband. But when he'd asked her to marry him, he'd said he understood that the grand opening would take an enormous amount of her time. She'd explained to him how it would be. It wouldn't last forever, just one more week.

And then she reflected on the night a week after he'd popped the question and asked her to attend the event with him. He'd cleaned, and prepared a candlelight dinner to celebrate their engagement, asking nothing of her but time to relax with him in return.

What had she done to enhance their marriage, to strengthen the bond between them?

She'd let her husband down.

Jonathan's trip had been a success. The only blight was that the situation was still unsettled between Johanna and himself. Between his own meetings and Johanna running around with the opening, he'd been unable to reach her while he was away.

He glanced at his watch. The plane trip from Asia was the longest he'd ever taken.

At least he would arrive in Nottoway in time to attend the opening.

Jonathan leaned his head against the headrest. He'd overreacted the night before he'd left town, but disappointment had ridden him when he'd sat without her at that table on the stage, the chair designated for her empty. He should have been more understanding, more patient with his new wife.

But sometimes it seemed the marriage was second in importance to her—behind the hotel. He under-

stood her need for success and he should have understood her drive. After the opening, he was sure her
schedule would free up to include them.

It wasn't so very long ago when he'd started his
own business. In hindsight, he could understand the
long hours, the hang-ups, the tension and the exhilaration of seeing it all come together. And tonight, it
would all converge to provide a success for his wife.
He only hoped they would have just a few minutes
to clear the air before the festivities began.

He'd been uneasy all week with the estrangement
between them.

Wasn't it said, never go to bed with an argument
unsettled, because the tension drained away the very
breath from a marriage? Too many nights of unspo-
ken discord, and distance could drive a couple in
separate directions. Eventually, neither party would
care one way or another about the other.

Jonathan vowed never to let that happen with
Johanna and him.

Jonathan drove directly home from the Richmond
airport. Once there, he showered and took the tux
out of the closet. Johanna had had his shirt cleaned,
thank goodness.

He'd just jerked one hand through the shirt sleeve
when the phone blasted. With one sleeve still dangling, he plucked up the receiver.

"Jonathan." He immediately recognized James'
voice.

"Yeah?" He held the phone with his ear and shoulder while he awkwardly reached for the other sleeve
and shoved his hand through.

"We've just caught someone in the act of switching
filters," James said.

Jonathan stopped dressing and caught the phone with his hand. "Who was it?" he barked, wondering if it was Alex Colfax, Sheryl's lover. He held his breath.

"Ronald Newton hired a Milton Holloway six months ago to work in his department."

"He didn't go the usual route through personnel?" he asked.

"No, Newton recommended the man."

Jonathan planted a hand on his hip, and paced, his shirt still hanging open. He glanced at his watch and kissed the few minutes he'd planned to spend with Johanna before the opening good-bye. "Have you talked to Newton yet?"

"Not yet. We haven't been able to reach him."

"Did Holloway implicate Newton? Did the man say why he made the switch?"

"He's not talking. Phoenix has him at the sheriff's office right now. Damion's going through his background, but hasn't found anything out of the ordinary so far."

"Has he worked in the field before?"

"He'd worked with another competitor but not Tri-Parts. He held a different position with the other company. So we don't even have that connection."

"Well, keep digging." Jonathan said, frustrated at the progress.

"Are you going to make it to the opening?" James asked him.

"Yes. Aren't you?"

"Of course. Damion will stay here. I've left the hotel's number in case he needs to reach either of us."

"Good. I'll see you soon." He disconnected.

More loose strings left an unsettling feeling in Jonathan's stomach as he buttoned his shirt. Glancing at the wall clock, he realized he had to rush if he planned to make it to the hotel by six.

He wouldn't disappoint his wife on this special night.

CHAPTER 16

Johanna's heart stopped when Jonathan walked into the hotel at one minute after six that evening. He was dressed good enough to make her faint. She'd wondered all week if he'd show up at all.

A staccato rhythm pounded in her chest when he neared her, kissed her lightly, and embraced her in a discrete hug.

Johanna closed her eyes. "Welcome home," she whispered through trembling lips, then she squared her shoulders. She couldn't get emotional right now.

Jonathan let her go when someone called her name.

Reluctantly, she answered the summons and watched him melt into the crowd, entertaining a businessman he knew.

Johanna turned her attention to the guests piling into the lavishly decorated hotel.

An array of exotic and palatable food and decorations were displayed.

Travel agents and local corporate sponsors traveled from as far north as Washington, DC, Baltimore and Richmond, and as far south as Raleigh and Charlotte, North Carolina.

Nottoway's own citizens attended the event in droves.

Elaborate ice carvings, artistic creations in themselves, riveted the gaze of every passerby. The carvings rivaled those of the best cruise lines.

Many political figures were in attendance, even the African-American governor of the state of Virginia. The mayor hobnobbed with a congressman, and a senator, who'd driven into town for the event bringing friends with them.

Representatives from large corporations in Richmond, Petersburg and Hopewell were in attendance. Anyone and everyone in need of hotels with meeting facilities was present.

In a corner of the lobby, a band played jazz low enough to allow the guests to converse politely. Inside the lounge, the more hip crowd danced to top fifty hits. Outside, near the pit, another group munched on barbecue and listened to soul music. In the conference rooms concert music serenaded them.

Waiters and waitresses kept the trays filled with food as they moved from room to room in their rented tuxedo-like uniforms.

In her tuxedo jacket and long skirt, Nicole was in her element, handing out the elaborate brochures made for the occasion and escorting some of the guests to displays featured in the hotel.

Johanna dazzled them all in a long, shimmering, royal blue gown with a scoop neck.

Patrick's sculptures added the piéce de résistance to the event. John Delecort, curator of the major art museum New York had asked Patrick to contact him about displaying some of his pieces at the museum. He also alluded to a major showing of his unique artistry in a friend's gallery in the fall.

Patrick had almost fainted. Johanna quickly guided him to a chair.

Delecort had remained in the gallery, studying the sculptures most of the night.

The elaborate presidential suite was on display until nine. Pam had booked it for ten that evening, and housekeeping needed time to clean it before the guest checked in. Johanna didn't know which corporation had booked the suite.

Henry escorted Gladys to the opening. She had walked around the place in high heaven, parading as the queen's mother, if not still a little miffed at Johanna because she'd refused to discuss Jonathan with her.

Pam and the sales staff busily booked appointments and boasted the hotel's stellar features to prospective clients.

At eight, Jonathan pulled Johanna aside to say he had to leave, but would return later.

Johanna wondered what could possibly take him from her tonight, but wasn't given long to dwell on it.

Ronald Newton had finally arrived at the company and was holed up in an office in the administrative building.

It took Jonathan and James ten minutes to reach the office from the hotel. Jonathan asked James to call Granger, the company's lawyer.

When Jonathan advanced into the room, Damion left, closing the door behind him, leaving Jonathan and Ronald Newton alone.

Jonathan sat on the edge of the desk. "I wanted to ask you about one of your employees, Milton Holloway," he said.

The older man nodded.

"I see that you recommended him for a position. How did you come to know him?"

"He went to school with Sheryl and he had some experience with working with airplane parts. He knew the business." Then he glanced, puzzled at Jonathan. "Is something wrong, Jonathan? He did good work. Always showed up on time. Didn't take time off for foolishness."

"We do have a problem," Jonathan said.

"What is it, Jonathan?" the older man asked.

How did one approach a man who'd always done well by your company. One who looked at you with innocence pouring from his eyes?

"Milton was caught switching defective engine filters for the good ones."

"No!" Ronald pressed his back against the seat.

"We need to know why and who else is involved."

"I had no idea? What did he say?"

"Nothing so far. But you're his manager. I thought you may have seen something strange."

He threw a suspicious glance at Jonathan. "You don't think I had anything to do with this, do you?"

"No. You've done a magnificent job for me from the very beginning." And Jonathan couldn't believe that this man had anything to do with the illegal parts.

A quick rap sounded on the door before it opened and James tucked in his head.

"Jonathan, Holloway's lawyer's here."

"Has Granger arrived yet?" he asked.

"He's waiting with the other lawyer."

Jonathan glanced at Ronald. "Excuse me a

moment, please." Jonathan left the room and joined the lawyers.

Once everyone was seated, Holloway's lawyer said, "My client is willing to disclose the person who hired him if you will drop all the charges against him." He waited for a response from Granger.

"Give my client something to work with. We're talking serious charges here."

"Let's say, you lessen the charges."

Granger looked at Jonathan and he nodded.

"Okay," Granger said, "talk."

Jonathan and Ronald entered the Newton's modest, but sparkling and nicely decorated ranch home an hour later. A light had been left on in the foyer for Ronald's return.

"Is that you, Ron?" his wife called out from another room.

Ronald immediately went to the couch and sank into the cushions like a man with the weight of the world on his shoulders.

"Susie," he called out in a weary voice, "can . . . can you come here, please?"

"I was baking an apple pie . . . " In a moment the woman appeared with a kitchen towel in her hand, but she stopped talking when she noticed Jonathan.

"Well, hello, Jonathan. Have a seat. You know we don't stand on ceremony here."

"Come on, Susie. Sit here beside me," Ronald said to his wife. He doted on her.

She sat next to her husband. "Don't you look handsome tonight," she said to Jonathan.

"Thank you," Jonathan answered, his throat tight. She must be sick.

Ronald covered her hand with his own wrinkled ones. "Honey, why'd you do it?"

She looked from Jonathan to her husband. "What are you talking about?"

"We know. Milton told everything. Why?" His eyes pleaded with her.

By degree, her eyes grew as cold as ice chips, as she glared at Jonathan. "You've got no right to be happy with that child when you put our baby in her grave!" Her tone was low but the intensity of her words cut to the bone.

Ronald's shocked gaze met his wife's. "Honey what are you talking about? Jonathan didn't cause the accident. He was nowhere around."

"He called off the wedding. Was going to shame our baby before the whole town."

Ronald's shocked glance met Jonathan's. "Call off the wedding? You talking crazy. Tell her Jonathan."

She nodded. "He called it off, all right."

"She talking crazy, isn't she, Jonathan? Why would you call off the wedding? It was going to be a grand wedding. Sheryl bought that pretty gown. I bought a new suit." He glanced at his wife. "Honey you even bought yourself a pretty dress to wear to the wedding."

"Just because Sheryl saw a friend that night is why."

She kept her eyes on Jonathan. He never knew that she'd hated him so much.

"What friend, Susie?" Ronald raked a hand over his bald head.

"Alex."

"That no account . . . What was she doing with him?"

She finally looked at her husband and clutched at his hands, tilting her head to the side. "It didn't mean a thing, Ronnie. It was just one . . . "

Ronald reared back as if the words had landed in a punch. "Woman, what are you talking about?"

"She was so pretty. And it was just one weak moment," she said in a small voice. "It wouldn't have happened again. Honest."

Honest. That was the same term Sheryl had used. *Honest.*

Tears trickled down Susie's lean cheeks.

"I'm sorry, Ronald. I didn't think you or your wife knew," Jonathan said from across the room.

Then Susie threw daggers with her eyes at Jonathan. "She came back here. But I made her go talk to you. I sent . . . " she covered her mouth with both hands as tears silently streamed down her cheeks, and she leaned on her husband's shoulder.

Her husband held her in his arms, silent tears trickling down his own cheeks.

"Don't send her to jail, Jonathan. I just . . . "

"I couldn't do that, Ronald. Don't worry about that." Jonathan couldn't bear their pain, and he glanced away. What justice could be served by adding more pain to a festering wound?

By ten, Jonathan hadn't returned and the opening was officially over. Many guests who had booked a room in the hotel, using the discount price offered for that night only, retired to the lounge to dance and drink the night away.

Although some food was left on one table in the lobby, all the other tables were discreetly broken down, the hotel restored to its usual stately self again.

All was done by eleven-thirty when Johanna was ready to leave her office. Pam grabbed her before she could escape.

"Johanna, I have to go, but you need to go to the

presidential suite. There's a problem you need to solve.''

"What's wrong?"

"I don't know, but the guest was raving about something. Please take care of it. He's one of our largest corporate clients.''

"What's his name and company.''

"A Mr. Speck. I forgot which company. Just go before he blows a fuse.'' She pointed her toward the elevator. "Don't dawdle.''

"All right.'' Johanna couldn't afford to have a client who paid that much for a suite dissatisfied with the hotel's services.

She took the elevator to the fifth floor. The door opened silently to display a table across from the elevator that held an elaborate floral arrangement.

She walked quietly down the carpeted hallway, taking note of the perfectly aligned prints hanging on the wall. When she reached the presidential suite, she knocked softly on the door and heard a muffled, "Come in.'' She twisted the knob. It was unlocked. Cautiously, she stepped into the room.

"Hello?" she called out.

"On the balcony.''

Puzzled Johanna walked through the living room where the balcony door had been left open. The balcony extended to the master bedroom and the living room in this suite.

A warm breeze ruffled the partially drawn draperies. Johanna parted the draperies and advanced through the door, and stopped.

Jonathan leaned against the high railing.

"You're here,'' was her lame response.

"Congratulations. You were a smashing success,'' he said. He held a glass of wine in his hand.

Johanna didn't quite know how to take his statement. Her visions of him lifting his glass of brandy to his lips in disappointment were unpleasant, and the memory reminded her that they hadn't resolved their problem.

"Come here," he said, setting his glass on the table and opening his arms for her.

Cautiously, Johanna advanced toward him, and he closed his arms around her, squeezing her. "I've missed you, sweetheart."

"Oh, Jonathan," She threw her arms around his waist. "I've missed you."

"Forgive me for acting a chauvinist pig before I left?" he mumbled in her hair.

"It was my fault. I shouldn't have forgotten."

"You had so much on your mind. And you did remind me of how frantic I was when I opened Blake Industries. I should have understood." He held her tighter. "It's just that I didn't think I'd grow to love you so much, and although I knew you loved me, I wondered if you could love me as much. I'm embarrassed at the weakness."

"Jonathan. I love you above all. The hotel is a material possession, but you," she whispered, stroking his face, "you're my heart and soul."

"Let's go inside and talk."

Arm in arm, they strolled to the living room and sat on the sofa. He told her about the Newtons, but Johanna's shock couldn't stem the streak of anger that swelled within her like a living thing.

"Why didn't you tell me?" Johanna asked. "Didn't you trust me enough?"

"Of course I trusted you, but I'd closed that part of my life, and I'd promised myself that it wasn't important any longer. But it was. I've looked at every woman I've dated and wondered if it was me she wanted or my money. I don't mind sharing, but I wanted a wife who I knew cared about me, and could understand my needs, wants and desires.''

Johanna wasn't appeased just yet. "Go on."

"I remembered all our conversations together, your dreams and mine. And we'd always connected. I trusted you, it's just that after being cautious for so many years, I was afraid to trust my judgment again."

Then he smiled. "And then, the day you returned to Nottoway, and I saw you by the river, Johanna, I was speechless. You knocked me off my feet. You weren't a teenager any longer. I had no protection against you and I couldn't stay away."

"You make me so angry," Johanna said.

"Don't, sweetheart. I love you more than you'll ever know."

Johanna peered at their entwined fingers. "I'll never be a socialite even though I'll participate in social obligations for our businesses."

"If you were, I wouldn't love you the way you are."

"Oh," she proclaimed, "I love you—always have."

"Forgive me for missing part of your opening?"

"You're here now. And I'm taking more time out for my husband."

"Your husband needs you," he whispered, heating her blood to a slow boil. "Let's try out that new bed that hasn't been used yet."

"We can't do that. We've got to go home."

"The suite is ours for the night."

"You're kidding?" A hopeful light appeared in her eyes.

"A change in location is good for a marriage, I'm told." He slipped his hands around her and unzipped her dress.

"And how did you become such an expert?" she asked, unbuttoning his shirt.

"I'm experimenting. Tell me in the morning if I was right."

"I love to experiment." She nuzzled his neck, knowing they had an entire lifetime to experiment together.

ABOUT THE AUTHOR

Reared in a small town in Southern Virginia, best-selling author Candice Poarch portrays a sense of community and mutual support in her novels. She firmly believes that everyday life in small town America has its own rich rewards.

Candice currently lives in Springfield, Virginia with her husband of twenty-two years and three children. A former computer systems manager, she has made writing her full-time career. Candice is a graduate of Virginia State University and holds a Bachelor of Science degree in physics.

Dear Reader:

Intimate Secrets was written in response to many letters asking me to tell Jonathan's story. I hope Johanna and Jonathan leave a warm place in your heart.

I love working with characters who realize their long-term dreams and goals. It leaves me feeling that anything is possible. Made the hero of his own story, Jonathan surprised me. What I had conceived at the beginning changed dramatically during the development. I was also very surprised by the identity of the villian, but the story took on a life of its own.

This novel was planned as the last in the Nottoway setting. However, recently I received a request to tell Kara's story after she grows up. Will I write her story? Only time will tell.

In the meantime, I'm working on my next release (untitled as of now) set in Maryland and scheduled for March 2000.

Thank you for so many kind and uplifting letters, and thank you for your support.

I love hearing from readers. You may write to me at:

P.O. Box 291
Springfield, VA 22150

or visit my web page at:

www.erols.com/cpoarch

With Warm Regards,
Candice Poarch

COMING IN OCTOBER . . .

FOOLS RUSH IN   (1-58314-037-9, $4.99US/$6.99CAN)
by Gwynne Forster
When Justine Montgomery discovers that her long-lost daughter
has been adopted by journalist Duncan Banks—and that he's
looking for a nanny—she enters into a web of deceit and divided
loyalties with her new employer. Their fragile trust and unexpected passion force them to risk everything to claim a love they
never thought possible.

SECRET PASSION   (1-58314-042-5, $4.99US/$6.99CAN)
by Layle Giusto
Stalking-victim Julia Smalls moves to Chicago to start a new life—
one without terror. Her boss is suspicious of her secrecy but no
one can deny their sizzling attraction. When strange accidents
start happening, Julia believes her past has come back to haunt
her and must make the choice between her life . . . and the love
of her life.

FALSE IMPRESSIONS   (1-58314-038-7, $4.99US/$6.99CAN)
by Marilyn Tyner
After Zoe Johnson stumbles onto a plot to steal high-tech soft-
ware, she unwittingly becomes the inventor's hostage. He thinks
she's a thief . . . but she thinks he's stunningly attractive. As the
weeks go by, both the truth and an unexpected desire unfurl as
the couple are thrown into a perilous game that could rob them
of their lives—and their love.

A SURE THING   (1-58314-048-4, $4.99US/$6.99CAN)
by Courtni Wright
ER physician Katherine Winters finds she must compete bitterly
with Thomas Baker for the chief of staff position at her hospital.
Yet she can't help being fiercely drawn to the attractive doctor.
For his part, Thomas finds Katherine irresistible. Can their desire
melt bitter rivalry into sweet love?

*Available wherever paperbacks are sold, or order direct from the Pub-
lisher. Send cover price plus 2.50 for the first book and $.50 per
each additional book for shipping and handling to BET Books, c/o
Kensington Publishing Corp., Consumer Orders, or call (toll free) 888-
345-BOOK, to place your order using Mastercard or Visa. Residents
of New York, Washington D.C., and Tennessee must include sales tax.
DO NOT SEND CASH.*

WARM YOUR SOUL WITH ARABESQUE . . .
THESE ROMANCES ARE NOW ALSO MOVIES ON BET!

INCOGNITO   (0-7860-0364-2, $4.99/$6.50)
by Francis Ray
Erin Cortland, owner of a successful advertising firm, witnessed
a horrifying crime and lived to tell about it. Frightened, she runs
into the arms of Jack Hunter, the man hired to protect her. He
doesn't want the job. He left the police force because a similar
assignment ended in tragedy. But when he learns that more than
one man is after her and that he is falling in love, he will risk
anything—even his live—to protect her.

INTIMATE BETRAYAL   (0-7860-0396-0, $4.99/$6.50)
by Donna Hill
Investigative reporter, Reese Delaware, and millionaire computer
wizard, Maxwell Knight are both running from their pasts. When
Reese is assigned to profile Maxwell, they enter a steamy love
affair. But when Reese begins to piece her memory, she stumbles
upon secrets that link her and Maxwell, and threaten to destroy
their newfound love.

RENDEZVOUS   (0-7860-0485-1, $4.99/$6.50)
by Bridget Anderson
Left penniless after her no-good husband turned up murdered,
Jade Bassett was running from the murderer whom she knows
was intent on killing her as well. On the streets of Atlanta she
had nowhere to turn to until she encountered successful graphic
designer, Jeff Nelson. Can she trust the handsome stranger prom-
ising to give her back her life?

*Available wherever paperbacks are sold, or order direct from the Pub-
lisher. Send cover price plus 50¢ per copy for mailing and handling
to BET Books, c/o Kensington Publishing Corp., Consumer Orders, or
call (toll free) 888-345-BOOK, to place your order using Mastercard
or Visa. Residents of New York, Washington D.C., and Tennessee must
include sales tax. DO NOT SEND CASH.*

THESE ARABESQUE ROMANCES
ARE NOW MOVIES FROM BET!

___*Incognito* by Francis Ray
    1-58314-055-7   **$5.99**US/**$7.99**CAN

___*A Private Affair* by Donna Hill
    1-58314-078-6   **$5.99**US/**$7.99**CAN

___*Intimate Betrayal* by Donna Hill
    0-58314-060-3   **$5.99**US/**$7.99**CAN

___*Rhapsody* by Felicia Mason
    0-58314-063-8   **$5.99**US/**$7.99**CAN

___*After All* by Lynn Emery
    0-58314-062-X   **$5.99**US/**$7.99**CAN

___*Rendezvous* by Bridget Anderson
    0-58314-061-1   **$5.99**US/**$7.99**CAN

___*Midnight Blue* by Monica Jackson
    0-58314-079-4   **$5.99**US/**$7.99**CAN

___*Playing with Fire* by Dianne Mayhew
    0-58314-080-8   **$5.99**US/**$7.99**CAN

___*Hidden Blessings* by Jacquelin Thomas
    0-58314-081-6   **$5.99**US/**$7.99**CAN

___*Masquerade* (in *Love Letters*) by Donna Hill
    0-7860-0366-9   **$5.99**US/**$7.99**CAN

Call toll free **1-888-345-BOOK** to order by phone or use
this coupon to order by mail.

Name _____

Address _____

City _____ State _____ Zip _____

Please send me the books I have checked above.

I am enclosing $_____

Plus postage and handling* $_____

Sales tax (in NY, TN, and DC) $_____

Total amount enclosed $_____

*Add $2.50 for the first book and $.50 for each additional book.

Send check or Money order (no cash or CODs) to: **Arabesque Books c/o
Kensington Publishing Corp., 850 Third Avenue, New York, NY 10022**

Prices and Numbers subject to change without notice.

All orders subject to availability.

Check out our website at **www.arabesquebooks.com**